WILD DECEIT

TYSON WILD BOOK FIFTY ONE

TRIPP ELLIS

Copyright © 2023 by Tripp Ellis

All rights reserved. Worldwide.

This book is a work of fiction. The names, characters, places, and incidents, except for incidental references to public figures, products, or services, are fictitious. Any resemblance to persons, living or dead, actual events, locales, or organizations is entirely coincidental, and not intended to refer to any living person or to disparage any company's products or services. All characters engaging in sexual activity are above the age of consent.

No part of this text may be reproduced, transmitted, downloaded, decompiled, uploaded, or stored in or introduced into any information storage and retrieval system, in any form or by any means, whether electronic or mechanical, now known or hereafter devised, without the express written permission of the publisher except for the use of brief quotations in a book review.

1

Red and blue lights flickered outside the house at 1485 Maple Park Drive. Several patrol cars were on the scene, as well as an ambulance and the medical examiner's van.

A crowd of curious neighbors gawked.

Paris Delaney and her news crew arrived just as we did.

We hopped out of the Plum Crazy Purple 1970 Barracuda, affectionately named the *Devastator*, and hustled across the lawn.

Camera flashes spilled out of the house as Dietrich snapped photos.

It was a small one-story with cream stucco and pale blue shutters. The roof looked a little haggard, and the lawn hadn't been mowed in a couple weeks. A lone palm tree presided over the grounds, and there wasn't much in the way of landscaping to keep it company.

Brenda hovered over the dead guy in the living room. She wore pink nitrile gloves and examined the remains.

The home was modest by Coconut Key standards. It had a spartan living room with a black leather couch, a ginormous flatscreen TV, a wooden coffee table, and a few plants to add life. To the right was a semi-open kitchen and dining area. The back door was through the laundry room. To the left, a hallway led to the guest bedroom, bath, and master bedroom. There was a small patio with a few pieces of wrought-iron furniture and a tiny backyard.

The two bullet holes in the guy's chest were the obvious cause of death.

Blood soaked the dark hardwoods. Pantyhose covered his face, making his head look like a potato. His cold brown eyes stared at the ceiling through the sheer nylon. A black 9mm lay on the ground not far from his right hand. A black backpack, dislodged from his left shoulder, was full of goodies—cash, jewelry, watches, etc.

Deputies Erickson and Faulkner talked to a frazzled woman in the kitchen. She was late 20s with long, dark reddish hair, mysterious blue eyes, and a slender frame with the right amount of curves. She had high cheekbones and intriguing features with a slim, long face.

A black subcompact 9mm lay on the kitchen counter.

It didn't take a brain surgeon to figure out what happened.

I flashed my badge to the woman as we stepped into the kitchen, and the deputies caught us up to speed on the finer points.

Deputy Faulkner introduced the woman as Desiree Jeffries. He said, "She came home and startled the intruder."

"I carry a gun in my purse," Desiree said, motioning to the pistol on the counter. "A pane in the back window was broken. I drew my pistol and entered the house. I saw him in the living room and..."

She didn't need to continue.

"You're lucky you weren't injured," I said.

"I'm not putting up with this shit."

"Have you had a break-in before?"

She nodded.

"Did you contact the department after that first break-in?"

"I did. It took an hour for a patrol unit to come out. I filed a report, but nothing came of it."

"What was taken during that first incident?" I asked.

She hesitated. "A little cash, some jewelry, various other valuables."

Faulkner said, "It's not uncommon for thieves to hit the same home twice after insurance has paid out. They know you'll be replacing the items."

Desiree's jaw tensed. "I'm just supposed to sit back and take it?"

"No, ma'am," I said. "Where were you prior to coming home?"

Her face tightened. "What does that have to do with anything?"

"I'm just trying to determine if you were routinely out of the house during this time. It's possible that the intruder had cased the premises and learned your schedule."

"I was with a friend," she said.

I noticed the ring on her finger. "Where's your husband?"

"He's at work. He's not usually home till late. One of the reasons I always carry a gun."

Her eyes were still wide with adrenaline, and she fidgeted nervously. I suspected it would take a while for her to wind down.

Brenda had removed the pantyhose from the intruder's face.

I said to Desiree, "I know it's unpleasant, but can you take a look at the intruder and tell me if you recognize him?"

She nodded and followed me into the living room. One glance at the corpse and her face tightened with rage. "That son-of-a-bitch!"

2

"I take it you know this guy?" I said.

Desiree growled. "He's a friend of my husband's."

That hung there for a moment.

JD and I exchanged a look.

"Maybe your husband should get better friends," JD said.

Desiree fumed with anger. "That fucker tried to kill me. This was a setup. They tried to make it look like a robbery and take me out when I came home. That's obvious to you, right?"

"I take it things aren't well between you and your husband?" JD asked.

She sneered at him. "Whatever gave you that idea, Sherlock?"

"We'll have a word with your husband," I said. "Where does he work?"

"The Pussycat Palace. He's a DJ. I want him arrested!" she demanded. Her jaw clenched tight, and her eyes burned. "You tell that bastard not to come home tonight. I've got something for him if he does."

"Let's de-escalate the situation," I said. "Right now, we have no reason to believe there was a conspiracy. Rest assured, we will do a thorough investigation."

Her eyes narrowed at me. "I was planning on filing for divorce. It's obvious he doesn't want me taking half his fucking money."

"I know you're upset right now, but I would urge you not to jump to conclusions."

"I'm not jumping to anything. I'm using my brain and putting two and two together. Hopefully, that's something you're capable of."

I remained calm. "I don't want to have to make a trip out here again for another shooting."

"That's why you need to arrest him and get him off the streets before he tries something like this again."

I knew better than to get into it with her. "Like I said, we'll talk to him and investigate this further."

"If he thinks he's gonna come back here and act like everything's hunky-dory, he's sadly mistaken."

"I'll relay the message. What's your husband's name?"

"Shane Jefferies."

"Are you sure he's at work right now?"

"That's where he's supposed to be."

"Can you tell me the intruder's name?"

"Knox Weaver."

Desiree was definitely hot under the collar. I didn't see her cooling down anytime soon. She called her husband's phone and ranted on his voicemail. "You son-of-a-bitch! You tried to have me killed!"

She went on for several minutes, cursing at him.

I took another look around, soaking in the details of the scene. Just as Desiree had said, a pane of glass in the back door had been punched through. Shards lay scattered inside on the tile by the door, consistent with someone breaking the glass from the outside.

Brenda and her crew bagged the remains.

Paris and her news crew were outside, picking up footage of the house and emergency responders as they stepped in and out of the home. The ambitious blonde reporter talked to a neighbor who "heard gunshots."

We left and headed to the *Pussycat Palace*.

Whether he was involved or not, Shane sure as hell didn't want to come home tonight. Desiree might accidentally shoot him on purpose.

Neon signage glowed, bathing the cars in pink and blue as we pulled into the lot of the seedy strip club on the edge of town. It was pretty full at this hour of the night. Sultry pop music thumped inside, oozing through the walls and spilling out of the main door.

The strip club wasn't as nice as *Forbidden Fruit*. The drinks were a little cheaper, and the regulations a little looser. The girls at Forbidden Fruit looked like they stepped out of the pages of a magazine. The Pussycat Palace was a little more... true to life. This magazine had been left in the backseat of a car in the sun and had beer spilled on it. But there were a few diamonds in the rough.

We stepped through the door, and I flashed my badge to the burly bouncer. "Looking for Shane."

The burly guy nodded toward the interior of the club.

We walked past the cashier and stepped into the den of debauchery. The place smelled like beer, cheap perfume, and desire. Spotlights slashed the hazy air, and girls pranced the stage in various states of undress. Stiletto heels stabbed the mirrored floor.

Bert, the manager, leaned against the bar, surveying his domain. He wore a tank top and cargo shorts and still had his hair trimmed in a mohawk. He was well past the age of retirement but had no intention of slowing down.

We moved through the club to the DJ stand. The booth towered above the floor. When the song ended, Shane leaned into the microphone. In a low, smooth voice, he said, "Please give it up for Whitney!"

There was a round of lackluster applause.

Whitney collected stray dollar bills from the stage and pranced away as the next beauty took the spotlight.

"Give a warm welcome for Mercedes!"

Shane spun up another tune. By that time, he had seen my shiny gold badge that I held in the air.

"When's the last time you talked to your wife?" I shouted over the music.

He looked at me, confused. "I don't know. This afternoon. Why? She in some kind of trouble?"

Shane had long, sandy-blond hair, green eyes, and a trimmed beard. He was early 30s and looked like he could play a sleazy bad boy on a soap opera. The kind of guy that nice women got mixed up with, even though they knew better. I had no doubt he had the eye of more than a few dancers, which probably put a strain on his marriage. If I had to guess, I'd say he probably met Desiree in the club.

"I guess you haven't checked your voicemail," I said.

"No. I don't answer the phone while I'm working."

"Someone broke into your house."

His brow lifted with surprise. "Really? What was taken?"

"Nothing."

He looked relieved.

"The intruder didn't make it out alive." I gave him the details.

"No shit?"

I nodded. "Your wife's a pretty good shot. I wouldn't want to be on the wrong end of her pistol."

He cringed. "I guess not."

"You know a guy named Knox Weaver?"

"Yeah. Went to high school with him."

"Your wife seems to think you hired him to kill her."

His brow crinkled again. "What!?"

I shrugged.

"That's ridiculous!"

"Are you guys close?"

"He comes in here every now and then. But it's not like we're drinking buddies. Why would I want to kill my wife?"

"You tell me."

He hesitated. "Look, things aren't the greatest at home. I'll admit that. If she wants a divorce, I'm all for it."

"Divorce is expensive," I said.

"So?"

"Probably be easier if she just disappeared."

He looked annoyed. "I don't think facing a murder charge would be easy. I like my freedom. Desiree has an active imagination."

"You been here all night?"

3

"Yeah, I've been here all night," Shane said. "And I got about a dozen witnesses, if you want to verify that. But what does that have to do with anything?"

I shrugged again.

"I don't know what to tell you. I didn't hire anybody to kill my wife."

"Well, you might not want to go home tonight," I said. "She seems pretty hot about it."

His face wrinkled, annoyed. "She's always pissed about something."

I dug into my pocket and gave him a card. "We may have more questions for you."

He frowned at us before we left.

We meandered through the club. Bert eyed us with curiosity and concern. Our investigations had taken us to the Palace before. He knew who we were, and I don't think he liked cops in the place.

I gave a nod to the bouncer as we stepped outside and strolled to the Devastator.

"You think there's anything to Desiree's allegations?" JD asked.

"There's one way to find out."

I pulled my phone from my pocket and sent a text to Isabella, my handler at *Cobra Company*. The clandestine agency had vast intelligent resources. Tracking cell history and call logs were child's play for her. And she didn't need a warrant. It wasn't exactly legal, and we couldn't use any of the information she gave us in a court of law, but it certainly came in handy from time to time.

I texted her Shane's phone number and asked her to see if she could find any connection between the DJ and Knox Weaver.

We hopped into the muscle car and slid into the white vinyl seats. JD cranked up the engine, and the exhaust growled. Music from the club still spilled into the parking lot as we rolled away and headed back into town.

We filled out after-action reports at the station. Isabella called back as we sat in the conference room, typing away on iPads under the pale fluorescent lighting.

"As far as I can tell, there are no calls between Shane Jeffries and Knox Weaver," she said. "Doesn't look like they kept in contact. If they did communicate, they did it through burner phones, met in person, or maybe email."

"Good to know," I said. "If there was a conspiracy, the whole thing could have been arranged at the club."

"I'll leave that for you to figure out. Anything else I can do for you?"

"Not at the moment, but I'll let you know."

"I'm sure you will."

We finished at the station, drove back to the marina at *Diver Down,* and stopped in at the bar to chat with Teagan. The teal-eyed beauty always had a cheery demeanor, and her tiny bikini top was uplifting.

She poured us two glasses of whiskey and had them waiting by the time our butts hit the barstools.

We smiled appreciatively and sipped the fine amber liquid.

It was still calm on the island. The Spring Break madness hadn't hit yet. But it wasn't far away. By this weekend, Coconut Key would be crawling with drunk college students looking to blow off steam. There would be an influx of petty crime, but hopefully, nothing too heinous.

The band got booked to play the Spring Fest at *Taffy Beach*. So much for the idea of escaping the season of madness and going on vacation. But Spring Break in Coconut Key certainly had its perks.

"Any word from your stalker?" Teagan asked JD.

JD's last fling had an *incendiary* personality. She set his Porsche on fire and almost succeeded in doing the same to him.

"She has proven to be rather elusive," Jack said.

There was a warrant out for her arrest, but she hadn't turned up.

"Her name's not even Veronica," he continued. "Apparently, she had stolen someone else's identity and racked up a hell of a lot of credit card debt, among other things."

"That chick was crazy," Teagan said.

"You're telling me."

"And you didn't pick up on the subtle clues?"

JD raised his hands innocently. "She seemed nice at first."

Teagan rolled her eyes. "You boys need to start thinking with the big brain."

Jack frowned at her. "I do think with the big brain."

She gave him a doubtful look. "Think harder."

JD dismissed the notion.

"She's dangerous, JD. She's still out there. She could still be fixated on you. What if she comes back, looking to finish the job?"

"She's long gone from here," he assured. "She ain't coming back."

"You know what her real name is?"

"Vanessa Hughes. She's wanted in three states for fraud, identity theft, and a few other things."

Teagan raised her eyebrows, astonished. "Geez!"

Jack shrugged.

"Your picker's broken."

"It's not broken. It just may be inaccurate at times." He grinned.

"All the time."

I laughed.

She shot me a look. "You can't laugh. You're just as bad."

"Me?"

"Yes, you."

"We are just innocent pawns in the game of love," JD said in a poetic voice. "Beguiled by angelic faces and sinful temptations."

Teagan rolled her eyes.

We sipped whiskey, shot the shit, and enjoyed the rest of the evening.

It was around noon the next day when I got a frantic call.

4

"Is this Tyson Wild?" a man asked, calling on *Memo*, an encrypted messaging app.

I wasn't big on calls from unknown numbers. "Who's speaking?"

"Owen Patterson." His voice shook. "Tony Scarpetti gave me your name. He said you could help. I think I've got a problem."

"How do you know Tony?"

"The card game."

Tony was a reformed Mafia guy who ran a high-stakes poker game at the *Seven Seas*. You had to have big money to get a seat at the table. And if you acted like a douchebag, you didn't get invited back.

"I'm freaking out," Owen said.

"Just slow down. Take deep breaths. Tell me what's going on."

Owen inhaled. "It's my girlfriend. She was supposed to fly into the FBO. I arranged for a car to pick her up. When the driver got there, she was gone."

"Maybe she took another car," I suggested.

"She hasn't called me. She won't answer the phone. I talked to the flight crew at the airport. They said she got into a limo and left."

"Maybe she used a different car service. Maybe the battery on her phone is dead. Maybe she got lost trying to get to you. Has she been to Coconut Key before?"

"No. I had my yacht brought down here, and I flew in a few days ago. We're planning on spending Spring Break here."

"Was she traveling alone?"

"No. I sent Maverick to escort her."

"Who's Maverick?"

"One of my bodyguards."

"Have you tried getting hold of him?"

"He doesn't answer either. This is highly unusual."

Judging by the fact that Owen had a yacht, knew Tony, had bodyguards, and could afford to fly his girlfriend private, I assumed he had resources. Big resources. That made him a target.

"Have there been any ransom demands?" I asked.

"No."

"Where are you at right now?"

"I'm on my yacht at Sandpiper Point."

"What's the name of the boat?"

"Diamond Hands."

It was a common name among crypto types.

"Alright. Sit tight. I'm going to contact the FBO and see if we can get surveillance footage. Maybe we can get a glimpse of your girlfriend as she left the airport." I paused. "If you hear anything, call me immediately."

Just as I was about to get off the phone, Owen groaned, "Oh, shit!"

"What is it?"

"I just got a text on Memo. They say they've got Skyler. How did they get my number?"

"I think these people know more about you than you can imagine."

I knew where this was going.

His throat tightened, and his voice trembled. "I'm supposed to await further instructions." He grumbled to himself. "Son-of-a-bitch!" His voice filled with panic. "They say if I go to the cops, they'll kill her."

Owen started to hyperventilate. I could tell he was pacing around, a nervous wreck.

"Who else have you talked to about this?"

"Just Tony. You're a cop, right? What if they know I'm talking to you?"

"They don't know. We're on an encrypted app. Unless they've got your yacht bugged or someone on the inside is leaking information, they don't know."

"Nobody is leaking information on my end."

"They knew your girlfriend was coming into town," I said dryly.

"That's 'cause she puts her whole life on the socials. I told her to stop doing that. No location pics until after we've left. And no hints about where we're going." An exasperated sigh slipped from his mouth. "That girl can't stay off her phone."

He broke down into sobs.

Through sniffling tears, he said, "They're gonna kill her!"

"They're not going to kill your girlfriend," I said.

"How do you know that?"

"If they kill your girlfriend, they won't get the ransom money, will they?"

He was silent for a moment, then muttered, "No. But they haven't asked for a ransom."

"They will." I paused. "It may seem like they're calling the shots, but you're the one who controls everything right now."

"I don't feel like I'm in control."

"That's by design. They want you panicked and afraid."

"Well, they've done a good job of that."

"All you have to do is stay calm and keep your wits. I promise I will do everything I can to help you get your girlfriend back. But you gotta listen to me."

"Have you done this kind of thing before?"

"Plenty of times."

"How does it usually work out?"

"When people in your position listen to what I have to say, it usually works out well. I'm not gonna blow smoke up your ass. These are unpredictable situations. But the key is to maintain leverage throughout the process. The minute they get what they want, you have no leverage. Understand?"

"Yeah."

"I need you to text them back on Memo and demand proof of life. If they're unwilling to do that, they don't have her, or she's already..." I didn't say it, and Owen didn't want to hear it. But we both knew what the alternative was.

His throat dried and tightened even more. "I love her man. You gotta promise me you'll do everything."

"You have my word."

"What about the FBI? Do we bring them in on this?"

"They're always willing to assist. But as of now, this isn't their jurisdiction."

He thought about it for a moment. "I don't want anybody else involved. I want to deal with you. Tony says you're the best."

"It's totally your call. I'll tell you, these guys are amateurs. This is likely their first kidnapping. Professionals know the authorities will get involved, and they expect it. And like I said, if they harm the hostage, they lose their leverage."

"Are you gonna come here?"

"I think you need to go about your life as normal. Right now, we have the element of surprise. Probably best to keep it that way. Don't give them any reason to suspect you've contacted the authorities. Who else is with you right now?"

"My two bodyguards. Leo and Jordan."

"Do you trust your staff?

5

Owen sounded confused by the question. "Yeah. I've vetted everyone myself. I trust my staff with my life. There have been plenty of opportunities where they could have screwed me over in the past. They've proven their loyalty."

"I assume you have access to cash," I said.

"Not cash, but crypto. That's what they want."

"I need you to text me the number they contacted you from. I'll put my people on it."

"People? I don't want anyone else to know about this."

"Trust me," I said. "My resources are secure."

He hesitated a moment.

"Look, I'll be honest. I doubt we'll be able to track them down. Kidnappers are getting more and more sophisticated about routing calls and covering their tracks."

After a moment, he said, "Okay. I trust you. You gotta understand. The sun rises and sets with her. She's everything. I'll do whatever it takes. Whatever the ransom is, I'll pay it."

"She sounds special."

"She is."

"Send me a picture of Skyler."

"I'll send you a link to her socials."

"I'll be in touch," I said before ending the call.

I filled JD in on the details.

"You know who that is, don't you?"

"The name sounds kind of familiar," I said.

"Owen Patterson is the CEO of XTC. It's one of the largest crypto exchanges. The kid is a multi-billionaire. It's no wonder his girlfriend was targeted."

A link to Skyler's *Instabook* buzzed my phone. I clicked the URL, and JD hovered as I scrolled through her profile.

I could see why Owen was willing to give up his fortune. Skyler was a knockout with several million followers. The sumptuous blonde had mesmerizing blue eyes, pouty lips, and elegant bone structure. She looked pretty damn good in a bikini or whatever you'd call the tiny threads of fabric that barely covered her all-natural endowments. Tan, glistening skin. Enticing curves. Alluring poses. Her feed was nothing but sexy pics in exotic locations, indulging in a lavish lifestyle.

There were no pictures of Owen.

I figured he was the one behind the camera most of the time. And nobody was following Skyler's profile to see pictures of her boyfriend.

That would ruin the fantasy.

Sure enough, there were several posts talking about her plans for Spring Break in Coconut Key.

We left the marina and headed to the FBO. We took a look at the security footage. Skyler and Maverick had willingly gotten into a black SUV that had pulled up to the plane on the tarmac. The license plate was not readable.

I called the limousine company that Owen had contracted. Someone had called and rescheduled the car to show up an hour later. I talked to the guy who took the call. "Was it a male or female who rescheduled?"

"Sounded like a woman."

"What time did the call come through?"

"Maybe half an hour before the flight was scheduled to arrive. Said they were going to be delayed."

"Do you have the number handy?"

"I can check the call logs. Hang on."

He put me on hold, then returned a moment later and told me the number.

It was the same number the kidnappers had used to call Owen.

I forwarded it to Isabella, and she tried to track the phone. As I suspected, the call had bounced through so many encrypted servers on the Internet that it was impossible to determine the origin.

"I'll monitor Owen's inbound calls, but I won't be able to get any info on the encrypted apps," Isabella said.

"Keep me posted."

We headed back to the *Avventura*. Just as we returned to the boat, Owen called in a panic. Through tears, he said, "They sent a video of Skyler."

"Is she alive?" I asked.

I put the call on speaker so Jack could hear.

"She's alive, but it's horrible. It was so hard to watch."

"Send me the clip. Did they make any demands?"

"They said I have 24 hours to transfer the entire holdings on the exchange, including my personal coins, to a crypto wallet."

"I hate to ask, but how much is that?"

He told me. The dollar amount was staggering.

"That's not pocket change," JD muttered.

"What do I do?" Owen asked.

6

"Don't release the funds until they release Skyler," I said. "Push for an in-person exchange. You want to make sure she is still alive and well when you hand over the money."

"But they specifically want the funds transferred to a crypto wallet," Owen said.

"Fine. But we make the exchange in person."

"I'll see what they're willing to do."

"The only way to get her back is to make them play by our rules. I need that wallet address."

"What are you going to do? Track it?"

"I'm gonna try."

It wasn't an easy task.

He sighed. "I'll let you know the minute I hear from them."

A moment later, Owen sent the video and the wallet address.

JD and I viewed the clip, looking for clues. It was hard to watch, and I didn't have a personal connection to Skyler. I could only imagine how Owen felt, seeing the love of his life bound and gagged, duct tape across her lips. Her mascara was smudged, staining her cheeks. Hogtied with rope around her wrists and ankles, she lay atop a bed. Judging by the sway of the camera and glimpses of the bulkheads, she was on a boat. At sea, she could scream as loud as she wanted to. There wouldn't be any neighbors to hear.

She was a little roughed up but generally in good shape.

There was nothing within the frame to indicate the date or time of the video.

I sent the clip to Isabella. She could pull the metadata and look for clues. Most photos and videos are automatically tagged with GPS data and camera settings. I didn't think sophisticated kidnappers would be stupid enough to send a file without stripping the information, but sometimes people overlook the obvious.

I texted Isabella the kidnapper's wallet address and asked her to run a background check on Skyler Graham's and Owen's bodyguards—Leo Bell, Jordan Wallace, and Maverick Jones.

Isabella called me back a few minutes later. "They all check out clean. No criminal records other than a marijuana possession charge for Skyler. All three guards have a military background. Maverick did a little MMA fighting. Was moderately successful. Looks like he's been with Owen for 18 months now."

"And the video clip?"

"No metadata. Sorry. I'll scan for background chatter and see if anyone is talking about the kidnapping. They're probably still in the area, but who knows for how long? Judging by the looks of that berth, you're looking for a sportfish or a small motor yacht."

"That's what I thought."

"I'll see what I can find out about that wallet address." She told me she'd be in touch and ended the call.

I was hesitant about our next move. We had a leak in the department. Paris Delaney seemed to know things as they happened. I trusted Denise and Sheriff Daniels. That was it.

I called the sheriff and filled him in. He didn't much care for it when we kept him in the dark.

"Shit," he grumbled at the news. "How do you want to handle this?"

"The client doesn't want to bring in any outside agencies."

"I can put patrol units on the water, looking for suspicious boats. We could do routine compliance inspections. Maybe something turns up. I can have Tango One spot from the air."

"I'll talk to Owen and recommend that path."

I ended the call, dialed Owen, and filled him in.

"I don't know. They said they'd kill her. I can't risk it."

"They get nothing if they kill her. Let us do our job," I said.

"You can't guarantee her safety."

"Nobody can."

He was silent for a long moment. With a hopeless sigh, he said, "Fine. Do what you think is best."

I ended the call and relayed the message to the sheriff. With any luck, the patrol boats would turn up something.

JD and I grabbed a late lunch at Diver Down and strategized, but we didn't have much to go on.

I talked with Owen again during the meal. He said he demanded the kidnappers make the exchange for Skyler in person, but he didn't get a reply. For now, all we could do was wait and hope we'd catch a break.

After we ate, we drove to Jack's house and picked up the Wild Fury van. The '70s era matte black van was decked out with chrome exhausts and Cragar S/S rims. It had an aggressive stance, a custom grill reminiscent of shark teeth, and plenty of special touches.

The beast snarled when JD cranked it up. It could lay the power down and paint the road with streaks of rubber.

We cruised to the distillery and picked up the first production run of Wild Fury Whiskey. We had burned through the test batch, and everyone seemed to love it. JD made a few minor tweaks, settled on a formula, and moved forward. We planned to unveil it with a soft opening at Diver Down. Spring Break was a perfect time to do it. The main launch would be at the Spring Fest. Since Wild Fury was headlining, it made sense to forgo our fee and sponsor the festivities. The logo would be everywhere. The liquor captured the essence of the band in a bottle.

If all went well, we'd roll out rum and tequila next.

We loaded cases of the stuff into the van and returned to Diver Down. JD had his distributor's license, so we could cut out the middleman and sell directly to retailers. It had cost a pretty penny, but was a smart move long term.

There was a decent-sized crowd, and Jack told Teagan to pour a round for everyone. There was much good cheer, and even Harlan cracked a smile.

Jack had an ear-to-ear grin as he watched total strangers enjoy his creation. We indulged ourselves and lifted our glasses.

"To good health, my friend," JD said.

We sipped the fine whiskey and reveled in our good fortune.

But the moment wouldn't last long.

7

"It's a blight on the community," Mary Connolly said. "It draws in a bad element."

JD scoffed, watching the interview on the flatscreen behind the bar. "Bad element. What a hypocrite!"

It was soft news for Paris, but a story was a story.

Mary Connolly was an outspoken 70-year-old woman with elegant features and stark white hair. She was a member in the Chamber of Commerce and involved in several other civic organizations. She played the role of an outstanding member of the community well. But we had it on good authority that she was moving up the ladder as a ruthless drug trafficker, responsible for the death of a teenage girl.

Unfortunately, we didn't have any hard evidence to support our assertions.

Mary seemed to be good at distancing herself from the day-to-day operations of her nefarious organization. With Hugo Ortega out of the picture, it left a power vacuum. Coconut

Key was a distribution hub that served the eastern half of the nation. Mary was eager to fill the drug kingpin's shoes, bringing in more and more of the cartel's product.

Mary was ranting about the Pussycat Palace and, to a lesser degree, Forbidden Fruit. At the edge of town, the Palace was the first thing tourists saw upon visiting the island. Her whole act was to deflect attention away from herself.

"It's poisoning our community," Mary continued. "These sexually oriented businesses have to go. They corrupt men's minds. Turn good family men into heathens. They're not safe. And I can only imagine what goes on behind closed doors."

I suspected she really didn't care one way or the other. It was pretty rich, coming from her.

My phone buzzed with a call from the sheriff. "I need you two to get over to the corner of Bluefin and Palm Grove."

I groaned. "What's going on?"

"Traffic accident. Witnesses claim a black SUV ran a vehicle off the road. Occupants are... Well, you'll see."

I informed JD, and we headed to the scene. Red and blue lights flickered, and firefighters doused a silver Lexus SUV with foam. There wasn't much left of the charred remains except the blackened shell of the vehicle. The acrid stench still lingered in the air, and the remaining hot metal popped and sizzled. The tires had melted from the rims and fused with the concrete.

The once silver Lexus had been forced from the street and plowed into the back of a parked car at the curb. The Lexus clipped the rear corner of the bumper, and the impact spun the vehicle. Bits of clear and yellow glass and plastic lined the roadway. The front end was an accordion, and both airbags had deployed. At some point, the vehicle burst into flames. The cabin of the car had been incinerated, and two bodies had melted into the seats.

It wasn't a pretty sight.

Cars slowed to a crawl, rubbernecking.

Pedestrians crowded the sidewalks, gawking.

Tango One pattered in the night sky, spotlighting the crash, bathing it in a bluish beam from the heavens. A news helicopter circled as well.

There were two fire trucks and an ambulance. Paris and her crew were already on the scene when we arrived.

Brenda examined the charred remains, and arson investigators tried to pinpoint the origin of the blaze.

Daniels looked on with a tight face. "Car is registered to Lauren Alexander. I'm assuming that's who's behind the wheel."

"Who's the passenger?" I asked.

The bodies were so badly burned, Brenda would need to track down dental records to confirm their identities.

"Husband, maybe," Daniels said.

The woman behind the wheel had a soot-covered diamond ring on what was left of her finger, which now looked like a charred curly fry.

Brenda moved around to the passenger's side and dug into the roasted man's back pocket. His bum against the leather seat had protected his wallet to some degree. The outer edges were seared, but Brenda was able to unfold the crispy wallet and pull out a half-melted driver's license. She squinted, trying to make out the name. "Dylan Reynolds."

"Guess that's not her husband," Daniels muttered dryly.

I looked around for a Department of Transportation camera and spotted one 50 yards away. With any luck, we would catch a glimpse of the accident.

The speed limit on the road was 35, but the impact indicated they'd been traveling at a much higher speed.

I talked to a witness that was on the sidewalk when the incident occurred. She said the black SUV was riding the tail of Lauren's car, then crossed the double yellow lines and forced her off the road into the parked car before taking off.

"It was definitely on purpose," she said. "This wasn't an accident."

"You're sure about that?"

She nodded, and her curly brown hair shook. "Positive."

I also spoke with a woman who was traveling in a vehicle behind the two cars. Her account was nearly identical to the woman on the sidewalk.

I got both of their names, then rejoined the sheriff.

"Maybe Lauren was having an affair, and her husband caught on," JD said. "Maybe he ran the couple off the road."

"Find out what kind of car he drives and go have a word with the gentleman," Daniels said.

"We're on it."

8

Denise texted me a picture of Lauren Alexander. She was a beautiful young woman with auburn hair, creamy skin, brown eyes, and classic features. She had a slight dimple in her chin and an air of mystery about her. She had lived with her husband in the upscale neighborhood of *Whispering Heights* in a two-story French colonial. The home at 425 Willow River Bend was surrounded by a white French Gothic fence. A large veranda with wrought iron patio furniture spanned the width of the house, and there was a large second-story terrace. Several tall, narrow palms dotted the yard, along with a short palm.

We parked the van at the curb, hopped out, and pushed through the gate. I was never a fan of doing death notifications. It was the worst part of the job. Made even worse when the significant other was a suspect.

It was a nice night, and a gentle breeze swayed the leaves of the palm trees. The moon hung low, and the stars flickered.

A moment after I knocked, a muffled voice filtered through the door. "Who is it?"

I displayed my badge to the privacy glass. "Coconut County. We need to speak with you."

Aaron Alexander pulled open the door.

He was not what I expected.

Aaron was a distinguished gentleman in his late 50s with coiffed gray hair, a square jaw, and blue eyes. He had the solid demeanor of a trusted news anchor. His confused eyes surveyed us. "What can I do for you?"

"I'm sorry to be the bearer of bad news," I said.

Concern bathed his face.

I said what I had to say in as direct a manner as possible.

Even the most rock-steady men go weak at news like this. The color drained from his face, and he looked a little wobbly. He grabbed the doorjamb to steady himself, and I thought for a second he might go down. He trembled as he asked, "What happened?"

I recounted the details, trying not to make it sound as grisly as it was. "It happened quickly. I don't think she suffered."

I may have stretched the truth quite a bit with that one.

He took a moment to process the information. His eyes were a million miles away. In a weak voice, he asked, "Where did this happen?"

He was asking all the right questions.

I told him the location.

Confusion knitted his brow. He shook his head in disbelief. "I don't understand. What was she doing there? She was supposed to be at a yoga class." The wheels turned in his mind. "That's not anywhere near..."

"I'm sorry, but I have more bad news. She wasn't alone."

His eyes snapped from that faraway land to me. "Who was she with?"

"We need to confirm his identity through dental records, but we believe the passenger in her car was Dylan Reynolds."

His jaw tightened, and I knew right away that he knew exactly who Dylan was. The color returned to his face, and sadness gave way to anger.

"I take it you're familiar with Mr. Reynolds?"

He took a breath. Through a tight jaw, he said, "He's a coworker of my wife's."

There was a moment of silence as he frowned.

"Can you tell me about the nature of their relationship?" I asked.

He drew in another deep breath and held it for a moment. "I know what you're thinking. Yes. The two were having an affair."

The fact of her infidelity wasn't surprising to me, but his knowledge of it was.

"I suspected something had been going on for a while now," Aaron explained. "A lot of late nights at the office. Long dinners and lunches. She grew... distant. I was in denial for a long time. I didn't want to believe it. But when your young wife stops having sex with you, it makes you wonder. She was always a very passionate woman. Then, more and more frequently, she found herself *not in the mood*. I'm sorry. I don't mean to burden you with the details of my failed marriage. But it led me to hire a private investigator. The truth was painful but not shocking."

"Can you think of anyone who may have wanted to run them off the road?" I asked.

His eyes narrowed slightly. "You mean, besides me?"

"Spouses are always suspects in situations like this. No offense."

"None taken. I'd be concerned if you weren't doing your due diligence. This doesn't sound like an accident to me. Perhaps an incident of road rage?"

"Perhaps. It seems people have a short fuse these days."

He gave a grim nod. "To answer your question. I was at home. Alone. I don't know what to tell you."

"What kind of car do you drive?"

"A black Escalade. Why?"

JD and I exchanged a glance.

"Witnesses claimed to have seen a black SUV run her off the road."

His face tightened with a grim frown.

"You mind if we take a look at your vehicle?" I asked.

"Be my guest. It's in the garage. If you'll give me a minute, I'll open it for you."

He backed away from the door and walked through the foyer into the living room. "Come on in. Make yourselves at home."

We stepped into the foyer and closed the door behind us, then followed him into the living room.

It was a nice place with light hardwood floors, cream walls, and color-coordinated abstract paintings on the walls. There was a sleek leather sofa and loveseat and a matching recliner that surrounded a glass coffee table. A large flatscreen display provided hours of viewing enjoyment.

It was an open floor plan, and the kitchen had Onyx countertops and stainless steel appliances. Aaron fumbled for the clicker to the garage door in a bowl on the counter. He pressed the button, and the rumble of the garage door filtered into the house. He motioned us into the kitchen and let us out the back door by the laundry room.

The overhead light illuminated the pristine vehicle. It had recently been washed, and the tires were slick with protectant. The garage had an epoxy floor that was immaculate. There was a small workbench and toolset on a pegboard with every item in its place. This was a guy who was meticulous about his possessions.

JD and I strolled around the vehicle, surveying the bodywork for damage. It looked like it had just rolled out of the showroom.

"Satisfied?" he asked, trying not to sound annoyed.

I nodded. "Like I said. Routine."

"No problem. I guess you don't have any leads at this time?"

"We'll review the Department of Transportation footage and see if we can enhance the images. As it stands, we're unable to determine the license plate number or exact make of the car."

He frowned.

"Did your wife have any enemies?"

"Not that I know of. But then again, there were clearly a lot of things that she kept from me."

"What about Dylan?"

"I didn't know the scumbag that well, only what my investigator was able to gather. And from what he gathered, Dylan was quite the ladies' man. My wife wasn't the only person he was seeing. I'm not sure if she was aware of that. I really couldn't tell you what was between them. I don't know if it was a fling or something more. Did she have real feelings for him?" He sighed. "I don't know. What's worse? Your wife screwing another guy just for variety or because she loves him?"

"Sucks either way," JD said.

Aaron's lips tightened, and he shook his head in dismay again.

"Where did your wife work?" I asked.

9

"ARMG Unlimited," Aaron said.

I recognized the name. "You said Dylan was a coworker?"

He nodded.

"That's a defense contractor," I said.

"Advanced Research and Materials Group. They make an array of products. Some of which are geared toward military and law enforcement. Of course, they have plenty of products geared toward consumer applications. A lot of the materials they develop crossover." He paused. "Do you think this could be work-related?"

I shrugged. "We'll cover all the bases." I paused. "Did this PI uncover any emails or text messages between the two?"

"He was able to hack into my wife's phone and her computer. There were several incriminating conversations. I think the majority of the time they used encrypted messaging applications to send voice memos, pictures, videos." Aaron looked distressed. The thought of it seemed to fill his mind with imagined images he'd rather not see. "Do I need to ID the body?"

"I'm not sure if that's possible. There was a lot of damage."

Aaron cringed.

"We'll need access to her dental records."

He nodded.

I gave him my card and offered condolences once again. I told him we would be in touch.

We left the garage and walked down the driveway, then strolled the sidewalk to the Wild Fury van. We climbed inside, and JD cranked up the engine.

"Poor bastard," Jack said in a sympathetic voice.

We returned to the station and filled out after-action reports.

I called Isabella and had her check both Lauren's and Dylan's call logs and get the GPS data for Aaron Alexander's phone. If he caused the accident, maybe he was dumb enough to take his phone with him.

"You hear any chatter about the kidnapping?" I asked.

"Nothing," she said. "I've sifted through the call logs on all the bodyguards, Skyler, and Owen. Nothing stands out. Skyler's phone hasn't appeared on the grid since she got into the limo at the FBO. Neither has Maverick's. I've gone over the proof-of-life video multiple times. I can't glean any useful information. Sorry, but I don't know where they've taken her."

"I appreciate you going the extra mile."

"Just remember that."

"I will."

Daniels pushed into the conference room. He had two bulletproof vests in hand. He tossed them onto the conference table and they slid across the wood.

"Gotta run," I said to Isabella. "We'll talk later."

JD and I examined the gear.

The body armor was sleek and thin, made from a breathable material that almost had a stretch quality. It was like a fitted tank top that could easily be worn under a T-shirt or duty uniform. State-of-the-art stuff.

"What's this?" I asked.

"What's it look like?" Daniels said.

"We already have our own."

"Now you've got a backup. We just got them in. Everybody gets one. Supposed to be the latest, greatest tech. Now you've got no excuse for not wearing one." He paused. "What do you make of the husband?"

I shrugged. "I don't think Aaron ran his wife off the road, but he's certainly got a motive."

I filled the sheriff in on the situation.

"No alibi, and he drives a similar car to what witnesses reported," Daniels said in a suspicious voice.

"Car looked clean."

"Dig into the guy."

"You know I will." I changed the subject. "About the kidnapping... Patrol boats find anything?"

"Nothing yet. They're stopping every vessel on the water that remotely matches the criteria. For all we know, they've taken Skyler to a remote location. I hate to say it, but I'm not optimistic about this one."

"Maybe they'll let her go if Owen pays the ransom," I said, knowing better.

He gave me a doubtful look. "As long as she can't ID them, she's got a chance."

The penalty for kidnapping in Florida is pretty stiff. It's a 1st degree life felony. For most criminals, murder is not much of a leap. Letting a hostage go means there is a witness. That is often a powerful motivator not to let a captive live.

We left the station and headed back to the *Avventura*. I called Owen along the way. "How's it going?"

"It's going. I mean, I'm trying to stay calm, but the kidnappers never responded. I'm starting to freak out. We're running out of time. What do I do if the deadline arrives and I still haven't heard from them?"

"Let's cross that bridge when we come to it."

"That's easy for you to say. I'm a nervous wreck. I'm not going to sleep at all tonight. Have you found out anything?"

"I've got people working on it."

"People? What are *you* doing?"

"I'm utilizing every resource I have available."

"You said you could handle this!"

"I can. I wish I had good news to share with you, but I don't."

"You said I was the one in control. I don't feel like I'm in control. I've sent them multiple texts, but they won't respond."

"Tell me about all of your enemies," I said.

"Too many to fucking count. You don't get to where I am without pissing off a few people."

"Start at the top."

He grumbled, agitated. "People lose their life savings every day. They gamble it all away, and markets can turn on a dime. Who do they blame? Me. Not themselves, but me. I just provide a platform for them to trade. If they do something stupid, it's on them. I get death threats all the time. But the platform has also helped create countless new millionaires. It takes patience, dedication, timing, and luck. If everything goes your way, you're on easy street. But dipshits buy all-time highs on leverage, thinking that the market can only go up. They get wrecked on the way down." He sighed. "Maybe a pissed-off client thinks he can squeeze money out of me."

"I'm guessing he probably can."

"I'm not going to let her die," Owen said.

10

"What's your risk tolerance?" I asked. I knew the answer.

"What do you mean?" Owen asked.

"They want the money as bad as you want your girlfriend back."

"I don't know about that. I want Skyler pretty bad."

"If it were me, I'd tell them if they don't respond, the deal is off."

"I'm not willing to do that."

"Maybe we should bring in other agencies. Notify the Coast Guard. Expand the search. The more people looking for Skyler, the better."

He hesitated, then sighed. "Okay."

"I think it's a good idea. We need all the help we can get."

"Look, I'm sorry for snapping at you. I'm just stressed."

"Don't worry about it. Understandable. Call me the minute you hear anything from the kidnappers."

"I will."

I called the sheriff and told him to bring the Coast Guard into the search. At this point, there wasn't much we could do.

We hung out at Diver Down for the rest of the evening, and JD hustled Wild Fury Whiskey on anyone that would take a free drink, which was pretty much everyone. The place was packed, and they sucked up the whiskey in no time.

The bar closed, and we hustled everyone out. There were plenty of stragglers who didn't want the party to end. It wouldn't be hard to find an all-nighter somewhere.

It was a little after 2 AM when the sheriff called with bad news. "If you two are still standing upright, I need you to meet me at the Pussycat Palace."

"Isn't it closed now?" I asked.

"This isn't a social call. Remember that DJ you talked to?"

"Shane?"

"He's dead."

My brow lifted with surprise. "Really?"

"Somebody gunned him down in the parking lot."

"We're on our way," I said before ending the call.

I caught JD up to speed, and he tossed me the keys to the van. He was pretty lit up. I think he downed a drink for every one he gave away, regaling potential customers with tales of the origin of the whiskey.

We hustled across the parking lot, and I climbed behind the wheel of the van. The engine growled as I twisted the ignition. JD fumbled to buckle his seatbelt, which proved to be rather challenging in his current condition.

I zipped us across the island to the strip club.

Patrol cars and emergency vehicles lined the parking lot. Lights flickered and flashed.

A crowd of curious onlookers gathered. Several dancers, the bouncer, the manager, and a few other employees loitered around, their faces twisted with shock and horror. Girls cried, and tears streaked their mascara.

We hopped out of the van and approached the carnage.

Shane lay on the asphalt not far from the exit.

Multiple gunshot wounds peppered his chest, and crimson stained his shirt and pooled around his body. The neon signage of the club reflected in the red, syrupy liquid.

Deputies kept the crowd at bay.

I pulled a pair of nitrile gloves from my pocket, snapped them on, knelt down beside the body, and checked for vitals.

Shane was long gone.

I'm sure someone had already checked, but I'd seen supposedly dead guys take a breath before. Sometimes the little things get overlooked.

I glanced around but didn't see any shell casings.

I stood up, moved toward the club entrance, and flashed my badge to the manager, Bert. "Anybody see anything?"

"I was inside the club." Bert pointed to the burly bouncer, Denver.

"Club was closed," Denver said. "Customers had mostly left. Shane didn't stick around. He stepped outside, heading toward his car. I was just inside the door when I heard the gunshots. By the time I looked out, he was already on the ground, and a car was speeding away."

"What type of car?"

"Black Camaro."

"You get a plate number?"

The burly guy shook his head. "It all happened so fast. I took cover behind the door frame. I mean, fuck that. I'm not getting shot."

There were several craters where bullets had hit the exterior concrete of the building. A few slugs remained embedded.

Brenda and her crew arrived, and Paris Delaney wasn't far behind. The sheriff pulled in shortly after.

"Anybody else see anything?" I asked Denver.

"I think there was a customer or two in the parking lot, but they didn't stick around."

"Did you get a look at the shooter?"

"Not really. By the time I looked outside, all I saw was the rear of the car speeding away."

Brenda approached the remains, snapped on a pair of gloves, and went to work.

"Alright," I said, addressing the crowd. Some had started to drift away. "Nobody leaves until I get a chance to talk to you."

"Did you know Shane well?" I asked the bouncer.

He shrugged. "I mean, we worked together. But it's not like we went out and had beers on a regular basis."

"Did you know he was having marital troubles?"

Bert still hovered nearby.

"I tend to stay out of other people's business," Denver said.

"Might want to talk to some of the dancers," Bert said. "Shane may have been married, but I don't think that quenched his appetites."

"Did he get into any recent altercations with anyone?" I asked.

"Not that I'm aware of." Bert paused. "You think his wife had a hand in this?"

"She seemed pretty convinced that Shane hired someone to kill her. You hear any gossip?"

Bert raised his hands innocently. "I just run this place. But you should talk to Lana and Honey." Bert discreetly pointed the two beauties out as they stood on the walkway under the awning, wiping tears from their eyes.

Honey was a delicious blonde that seemed to be taking it harder than the rest.

I gave Bert and the bouncer my card, then strolled toward the dancers.

JD weaved behind me.

I flashed my badge and made introductions. "Evening, ladies."

Honey continued to sob.

Lana was a leggy brunette with long, straight hair, smoldering caramel eyes, and smooth skin. Her black push-up bra squeezed her ample endowments. They had a magnetic quality.

They both stood in high heels, wearing almost nothing at all.

Honey lived up to her name. When not crying, she oozed sensuality. A petite little package begging to be unwrapped. Her golden skin and all-natural curves sparked impure thoughts. I'm sure she did well in the club.

"Tell me about your relationship with the deceased," I said.

The two girls exchanged a look.

Lana said, "We were just friends."

"Friends with benefits?"

"Is that any of your business?"

"I'm just trying to get a sense of who might have wanted to put a few bullets into Shane."

"It's his fucking wife," Honey blurted through sobs.

"Did she know you were sleeping with her husband?" It was obvious there was something between them.

Honey hesitated. "No. I don't think so."

"But you were close enough that Shane confided in you about his marriage troubles," I suggested.

Honey nodded.

I looked at Lana.

"We hooked up a couple of times," she admitted. "That was it."

"And that didn't cause any jealousy between you and Honey?"

She made a face like it was a silly question. "We're best friends. And that was before they hooked up."

"What about the three of you?" JD asked with a lewd grin, swaying slightly.

They both looked at him, annoyed. "Yeah. So?"

Lana's eyes narrowed with recognition. "Hey, you're the guy in that band, right?"

JD smiled.

Lana smiled back, her defensive demeanor softening.

I steered the conversation back on track.

"Was it just a casual thing between you?" I asked.

Lana nodded while Honey shook her head.

"It was a little more than casual for me." Honey's face tightened, and the tears flowed again. She shrieked, "I loved him."

Lana put her arm around Honey's shoulder, trying to comfort her.

"He said he was gonna leave his wife," Honey said through jerky breaths. "I was going to leave my husband."

And just like that, I had another suspect.

"Did your husband know that you were having an affair?"

Her eyes rounded. "No."

"Are you sure?"

"Positive," she said, adamant. "He'd have killed me if he found out."

I exchanged a look with JD.

"So, your husband's a violent man?" I said.

"No. I mean, he only hits me when he gets really pissed off."

"Oh, is that all?" JD said.

"What kind of car does your husband drive?" I asked.

"A black Charger. Why?"

"Oh, I don't know. I'm thinking maybe he had a motive to kill Shane."

Concern tensed Honey's face. "You're not going to tell him about me and Shane, are you?"

"I'm going to interview him," I said flatly. "You know where he was tonight?"

"I talked to him before I left for work. I couldn't tell you where he's been all night."

"Does he ever come up to the club?"

Honey shook her head.

"Boyfriends and husbands aren't allowed," Lana said. "It's bad for business. Causes too much drama."

"This looks like a lot of drama," I said dryly.

Honey sniffled, glancing at the corpse. She started to break down again.

"Did Shane have a beef with anyone?"

11

The dancers exchanged another awkward glance.

"Oakley," Lana said.

"Who's Oakley?" I asked.

"He DJs during the day."

"What was the issue?"

"Shane got all the prime shifts."

"Is that it?" I asked, sensing there was something more.

"Well, Oakley has a little thing for Honey."

My gaze turned to the sinful blonde. She looked a little embarrassed. "Did you two ever hook up?"

She hesitated for a moment, then shrugged. "Yeah, like once." Her face scrunched with disappointment. "It wasn't very good."

"Were you seeing Shane at the time?"

"We were talking. I mean, we may have hooked up once or twice at that point. I don't know. It's not like I was married to Shane."

Her marital status didn't seem to make much of a difference either way. I didn't comment, and I could tell JD had to bite his tongue. He continued to sway, and a strong breeze would have blown him over.

"Was there ever a physical altercation between the two?" I asked.

"They got into it once," Honey said. "Oakley found out that I had slept with Shane and got in his face. He pushed Shane. Shane pushed back. Oakley hit the ground. By the time he got up, Denver was all over him. That was the end of it."

"What about drugs?" I asked.

"What about them?"

"Was Shane into anything illegal?"

The girls hesitated a moment and exchanged another awkward glance.

"I mean, Shane liked to party," Honey said. "Everybody likes to party."

"You mean cocaine?"

Honey shifted and shrugged her shoulders. "Nothing major. A little coke, a little X, a little weed. No big deal."

"Was he dealing?"

Honey shook her head, and her blonde hair swayed from side to side.

I gave her a skeptical look.

"Shane was a good guy. He didn't deserve this," she said through sniffles.

"What's your husband's name?"

"Boston. Are you really going to talk to him?"

"I think that would be wise," I said in an understated tone.

"You can't say anything about the affair."

"Something tells me he already knows."

"There's no way," she said, confident.

I remained doubtful.

I collected Boston's information, along with the girls' contact info. I gave them both a card and told them to call me if they could think of anything else.

Dietrich snapped photos, and Paris and her crew interviewed Bert and the door guy.

JD and I rejoined Brenda as she finished her examination.

Daniels's narrow eyes surveyed JD as I caught him up to speed. "What the hell's his problem?"

"No problem here," JD said.

Daniels just shook his head. "He smells like a distillery."

"Just quality testing the product." He smiled.

"You look defective."

JD frowned at him.

"9mm," Brenda said. She pointed a few feet away. "Tire tracks are probably from the shooter's vehicle. I'll see if we can get a tread match."

"We'll track down his wife," I said.

"Keep him away from the public till he sobers up," Daniels said, glaring at JD.

JD scowled back.

I talked to Denver again. "Could you have mistaken the shooter's vehicle? Could it have been another make?"

Denver shrugged. "Maybe. Like what?"

"A Charger, perhaps?"

He thought for a moment. "I don't know. Maybe. I thought for sure it was a Camaro. But it all happened so fast."

Eyewitness testimony was notoriously inaccurate, and I suspected Denver huddled inside the club until long after the danger had passed.

I dragged JD back to the van, and we left the Pussycat Palace, heading for Desiree's house. It was after 3 AM at this point.

I parked at the curb and killed the engine. "Stay here."

"Why?"

"I'll handle this one."

JD's mouth twisted with another tipsy frown.

I hopped out and strolled the walkway to the front porch. There were no lights on in the house, and the street was quiet. Desiree's car was in the driveway—a red Civic. I didn't see a black Camaro anywhere nearby.

I knocked on the door.

There was no response for a few minutes.

I kept knocking, then a light finally flipped on. Desiree staggered into the foyer and shouted through the door. "What do you want?"

"Coconut County. I need to speak with you."

She unlatched the deadbolt and pulled open the door. Her sleepy eyes glared at me. "This couldn't wait till the morning?"

"I'm afraid not. I'm sorry to tell you this..."

I informed her of the situation.

She looked a little stunned, but not upset. Like receiving an unexpected gift. "What happened?"

"Shane was gunned down as he left the club."

I gave her the details.

She asked all the right questions, but she was still at the top of my suspect list.

"Do you have any leads?"

"Can you tell me where you were this evening?"

Her eyes narrowed at me. "I've been here all night. Why?"

"You were pretty hell-bent on putting a bullet in your husband earlier."

"I was angry, and that was just talk. Besides, he tried to have me killed."

"We haven't been able to verify that."

"I don't give a shit what you can verify. I know he hired someone to kill me. And I'll sleep better tonight knowing he's gone."

"Mind if I take a look at your pistol?"

Her face tightened. "I do mind."

"The lab will run ballistics on the bullets that killed Knox Weaver."

She stared at me with concern.

"They'll also run ballistics on the bullets that killed your husband."

"They're not going to match. If that's what you're getting at."

"You sure about that?"

"Positive."

"Can you think of anybody else who may have wanted to kill your husband?"

Her paranoid eyes continued to glare at me. "I'm sure there were lots of people."

"You'll need to come down to the morgue and make a positive identification."

"Can it wait till tomorrow? It's not like he's going anywhere."

"It can wait."

There was another long, awkward pause.

"Is that all?" she asked. "I'm tired, and I'd like to get a good night's sleep."

"That's all for now," I said. "Sorry to disturb you."

She closed the door and latched the deadbolt.

I strolled back to the van and climbed in.

Jack was sawing logs.

I cranked up the beast, and the engine rumbled. He didn't flinch. I put it into gear and rolled away from the curb.

At the marina, I woke JD from his slumber. His droopy eyes looked around. It took him a minute to figure out where the hell we were.

JD climbed out and staggered down the dock to the *Avventura*. I made sure he didn't fall into the water along the way.

We crossed the gangway, and Buddy bounced and barked excitedly in the salon upon our arrival. I slid open the door, knelt down, and petted the little Jack Russell.

JD stumbled through the salon, making his way to his VIP stateroom.

I took Buddy out for a quick walk before settling in for the evening.

In the morning, I called Isabella and asked her to track Desiree's cell phone.

Her fingers tapped the keys, and within a few moments, she had the information in front of her. She sifted through the data. "What time did the shooting take place?"

"Between 2:00 AM and 3:00 AM."

"Her cell phone was at home at that time, but it wasn't there all night. Looks like she spent most of the evening at the Roosevelt apartments. Looking through her call logs, there is a lot of communication between her and a cell phone that is registered to Theo Malone. Calls and texts at all hours of the day and night."

"Sounds like she had a little something on the side."

"That would be my guess."

"Can you tell me what kind of car Theo Malone drives?"

Her fingers tapped the keys. "A late model, midnight blue Camaro is registered in his name."

I perked up. "Could be our shooter. Where was his cell phone at the time of Shane's murder?"

She tapped the keys again. "His cell phone was at his apartment. Maybe he was smart enough to leave it behind."

"I think he just shot to the top of my list."

"Let me know how it works out."

"I will."

Bacon sizzled in a pan as I grilled breakfast. The aroma filled the galley and drifted throughout the boat. Coffee percolated.

JD staggered out of his stateroom with bloodshot eyes and tousled hair, looking pretty haggard.

"How you feeling?" I asked with a snarky grin.

"I feel great. Why do you ask?"

He was full of shit.

I chuckled and dished up a plate. We ate on the sky deck, basking in the amber rays of morning sun. Gulls squawked on the breeze. Jack nursed himself back to the land of the living by sipping on coffee and slowly putting away a ham and cheese omelet.

I caught Jack up to speed, telling him what Isabella told me. After breakfast, he got cleaned up, and we took the van to Theo Malone's apartment.

12

The Roosevelt was a mauve-colored building with orange Spanish tile roofing and white trim. The three-building, five-story condo unit surrounded a pool. Palm trees towered over the crystal-clear water.

There was limited covered parking.

We pulled into the lot and strolled to the lobby. I buzzed the property manager from the call box, and she let us in. We walked through the small lobby to the elevators and cruised up to the third floor.

It was a nice place. Not cheap. Nothing on the island was. Each unit had a balcony with a decent view. A few leggy beauties sunned themselves by the pool, reclining in white lounge chairs with royal blue padding.

I banged on unit #318.

Commotion rumbled inside, and a moment later, the peephole flickered as someone peered through. A gruff voice shouted, "Who is it?"

I lifted my badge to the lens. "Coconut County. Need to speak with Theo Malone."

Theo had priors for assault and possession. Didn't make him a murderer, but indicated he was capable of violence.

He unlatched the deadbolt and pulled open the door. His curious eyes surveyed us. "You don't look like cops."

JD said one of his favorite lines. "We're a special crimes unit."

"So, why are you talking to me?"

Theo had short, scraggly brown hair, a round face, narrow green eyes, and a short, slightly curly beard. He had multiple cursive tattoos across his brow and under his eyes. An intricate design painted his left cheek. These tattoos were a commitment, no doubt about it.

"You were with Desiree Jeffries last night," I said.

He hesitated a moment. "Yeah, so?"

"She left out that fact when we talked to her."

"Maybe she forgot."

"Are you that forgettable?"

His jaw tightened. "What do you want?"

"I'm sure you've heard the news that her husband was killed."

"Yeah, so? What's that got to do with me?"

I shrugged. "I don't know. Maybe she asked you to take care of him."

His brow crinkled. "What!?"

"She was in fear for her life. Maybe she begged you to kill him."

"Where do you get this stuff from?"

"Deep down inside, you wanted him out of the way."

"Do you just go around making shit up and accusing people, hoping to stumble onto something?"

I nodded. "Pretty much."

"How's that working out for you?"

"Pretty well, actually."

"I had nothing to do with Shane's death."

"You drive a similar car to the shooter's vehicle. Witnesses claim they saw a black Camaro. Could have easily been mistaken for a midnight blue one."

Theo shifted uncomfortably, and the muscles in his jaw flexed. "Look. I was here all night."

"Desiree left the apartment before the shooting. You had plenty of time to get to the Pussycat Palace, do a drive-by on Shane Jeffries. Hell, maybe she went with you. Maybe you left your phone at your apartment, drove her back to her place, then the two of you went to the strip club and took care of her problem."

"That's an interesting story, but it's not anywhere close to the truth."

"How about you tell me the truth?"

He forced an annoyed smile. "I told you the truth. I was here with Desiree last night. She left and went home."

"Mind if we take a look around your apartment?"

"I do mind."

"I can get a warrant. We can come back and search your place, search your car. Who knows what we might find?"

"If you think you can get a warrant, then get one. Until then, I'm done talking to you dicks."

He slammed the door in our faces and twisted the deadbolt.

We left the apartment building and headed to the station. I filled out an application for a warrant, and based on the similarity between his vehicle and the witness's statements about the shooter's vehicle, Judge Echols signed off on it. We were back at the Roosevelt with a tac team in no time.

I put another heavy fist against the door to Theo's apartment and shouted, "Coconut County! We have a warrant!"

Erickson and Faulkner smashed the door with a battering ram. Wood splintered, and the jamb snapped. The door swung wide, and the handle punched a hole in the sheetrock.

I stormed into the foyer, my weapon in the firing position. The team flooded in behind me.

There was a kitchen to the right of the foyer, which opened to the living room. The unit had white tile floors and beige walls. There was a blue sofa, a glass coffee table, and a small entertainment center with a 45-inch flatscreen display.

We cleared the area, then moved to the bedroom door.

It was closed.

I shouted through the door, "Coconut County. Come out, Theo!"

With the tac team in position, I kicked open the bedroom door, swung my barrel inside the room, and cleared the corners.

It was empty.

The sheets were rumpled, and a few dirty clothes littered the floor. There were a couple beer bottles on the nightstand next to the bed.

We flooded into the room, cleared the bathroom, and checked the closet.

Theo wasn't in the apartment.

Maybe our knock and talk had spooked him, and he decided to get the hell out.

We rummaged through the apartment, searching the nightstand drawers, the dresser, the closet, the cabinets, and every other place we could think of.

We didn't find a 9mm pistol, ammunition, or anything else incriminating.

Theo had a baggie of weed and a few grams of cocaine in a nightstand drawer. We stumbled across it within the scope of our search for a weapon. It was admissible, and we were able to get a warrant for his arrest.

Daniel put out a BOLO.

13

We drove across the island to find Boston Sweet. Honey and her husband lived in a small two-bedroom house on King Bird Lane. The pale blue home was surrounded by a white point-and-blank fence. The maroon vehicle parked in the red brick driveway looked like a combination of an SUV and a minivan. The house had white trim and a mahogany door. There was a nice veranda with plastic patio furniture. Two clusters of towering palm trees shrouded the house, and a moped rested in the courtyard. It was a quaint little home.

We pushed through the gate, stepped to the veranda, and knocked on the door.

Footsteps shuffled inside the house. Through the privacy glass of the front door, I saw a figure approach. The door opened, and I flashed my badge. "Coconut County. Are you Boston Sweet?"

His face tightened. "Yeah, what's this about?"

Boston was an imposing figure. He stood about 6'1" and had a thick, blocky head, broad shoulders, and a nose that had taken a few punches. Dark stubble lined his jaw. He had a hard face and brown eyes. In his mid-30s, he looked like a guy who didn't take shit off anybody.

"No cause for alarm," I said. "We just need to ask you a few questions about last night."

His face crinkled.

"I'm sure you're aware that Shane Jeffries was killed."

"Yeah. My wife told me. That's terrible. He was a cool cat. I always liked him."

That stunned us.

"Did you know him well?" I asked.

"I wouldn't say I knew him *well*. We met a couple of times. I didn't go to the club much for obvious reasons. But I knew him from when he DJ'd at Bumper."

"Where were you last night between 2:00 AM and 3:00 AM?"

"I was here, sleeping. I was off last night. Why?"

"Where do you work?"

"I bartend at Quarterdeck. I pick up a few odd jobs here and there. Handyman stuff, mostly."

"That your car in the driveway?"

"Yeah," he replied, embarrassed. "I need something that's got cargo space to haul crap around. It was cheap, and it runs."

"You own a gun?"

His suspicion grew. "Yeah. Why are you asking me these questions?"

"Just routine. Covering the bases."

"You think I had some reason to do a drive-by on Shane?" He asked as if the notion was absurd.

I shrugged.

"What reason would that be?"

"Is Honey around?"

"She's still asleep. She was pretty upset last night."

His curious eyes flicked between the two of us as he put the pieces together. "You're not suggesting…?"

"I'm not suggesting anything."

He took a moment to process everything.

"What type of gun do you own?" I asked.

"A 9mm. Why? What was Shane killed with?"

"I can't disclose that information," I said. "You mind if we take a look at your weapon?"

His face crinkled. "I don't think I like where this is going."

"We can come back with a warrant."

I knew we didn't have enough probable cause in this instance.

"Then get a warrant," Boston said. He paused, disturbed by it all. "Are you saying my wife was having an affair with Shane? And you think I found out about it and killed him?"

"I'm saying that's a conclusion one might jump to."

The muscles in his jaw flexed. "Mother fucker!" he grumbled.

The reaction seemed genuine. I think this was the first time he connected the dots.

"If you'll excuse me, I need to have a conversation with my wife."

He closed the door and stormed down the foyer.

I exchanged a glance with JD, and he lifted an amused eyebrow.

"I'd like to be a fly on that wall," he said.

We walked back to the van. Our next stop was Oakley Sherman's apartment, but a call from Owen interrupted things.

"I think I fucked up," he said in a frazzled voice.

14

I cringed. "What happened?"

"I didn't hear back from the kidnappers," Owen said in a panicked voice. "So I paid the ransom."

I winced. "How much?"

"All of it. I mean, I sent half at first. Then demanded we make the exchange in person if they wanted to get the rest. They never responded. I waited for another hour, then I just sent the rest of it. The deadline was approaching. They haven't released Skyler or Maverick."

"Where are you right now?"

"I'm on my yacht."

"We're on our way over."

"Have your people found anything?"

"The Coast Guard and the sheriff's patrol units are still looking. Nothing has turned up."

I ended the call, and we hurried to Sandpiper Point. Traffic on the island had picked up now that the influx of tourists began to arrive. The madness was upon us.

We strolled the dock, looking for *Diamond Hands*. There were plenty of yacht parties and gorgeous beauties prancing decks in teeny bikinis. Music pumped through speakers, and the festive atmosphere permeated the marina.

Sandpiper Point was home to tech moguls, celebrities, crypto millionaires, and some old-school money. There were superyachts and bluewater sailboats. Pricey toys for the elite.

Owen had a 142' *Affini* with sleek windswept lines, a navy hull with white trim, and large windows that bathed the salon and interior spaces in refreshing light.

For a billionaire, it was rather modest.

We crossed the passerelle to the aft deck and banged on the sliding glass door to the salon.

A big guy with a slick head, dark sunglasses, and a goatee greeted us. He looked like he could snap a man in half. He was about 6'3" and carved from granite. He wore a light gray suit with a white cotton shirt, black tie, and a matching pocket square.

I flashed my badge and made introductions. Mr. Granite's name was Jordan Wallace.

"Owen is expecting you," he boomed.

Mr. Granite motioned us inside, and we followed him through the salon. We stepped through the hatch to the side deck and made our way up to the foredeck.

Owen sat on a settee next to a table, talking on the phone.

Another bodyguard, Leo Bell, hovered nearby. He wasn't quite as big as Mr. Granite, but he looked formidable. He had a hipster beard and trimmed hair. At 5'11", he was stout and had shoulders like bowling balls. Dressed in a gray suit, he matched his counterpart. A flex of the biceps could have torn the fabric.

There was no mistaking these guys as security.

Owen ended the call and stood up to greet us with a handshake. He was in his mid-20s with short curly brown hair, a round face, and worried blue eyes. His pudgy body looked like it hadn't seen the gym, ever. "Thanks for coming." His distressed eyes darted between the two of us. "I don't know what to do."

"You still haven't heard anything?" I asked.

He shook his head. "Nothing."

"How much money did you transfer?"

"Everything I could get my hands on. It was exactly what they asked for."

"Crypto transfers can take time," I said. "Sometimes up to several hours."

"I know. That's why I wanted to do it ahead of the deadline, just to make sure."

"Don't go to the worst-case scenario just yet."

His eyes filled. "I just don't know what I'm going to do without her. What if she saw their faces? What if she can ID them? They'd have to kill her, right?"

His face quivered, and he was on the verge of a breakdown.

"What did I just say?"

"Don't go to the worst-case scenario," he muttered, then grumbled to himself. "I'm such an idiot."

I called Isabella. "Any luck figuring out who's connected to that crypto wallet?"

"I'm using every trick in the book, but I can't connect it to an IP address or anything identifiable. Somebody's been careful."

"Any other chatter?"

"Nothing."

I told her the ransom had been paid.

"Is anybody listening?"

"Just me." I stepped away for some privacy.

"You want my honest opinion? Those kidnappers are long gone, the girl's dead, and so is her bodyguard. Nobody's ever going to find the bodies."

"You're full of optimism today."

"It's just a realistic assessment of the situation. These guys have covered their tracks. And they could be halfway around the world by now."

"I'll be sure to call when I need an uplifting pep talk."

"Any time. I'm here to help."

I ended the call.

Owen's wide eyes begged for information. "That didn't sound good."

"Sorry. No luck tracking down the wallet, but my people are trying."

Owen paced the deck, a nervous wreck.

A message buzzed his phone.

He pulled the device from his pocket and swiped the screen. "It's from them," he said, glancing at us with terrified eyes.

The color drained from his tan cheeks.

15

Owen's finger trembled as it hovered over the playback icon of the clip. "I don't know if I want to watch."

He pressed play, and it quickly became clear that this was a video he should never have seen.

Tears streamed down Skyler's cheeks. She was still bound and gagged. She was on her knees, and the kidnapper behind her grabbed a fistful of her hair. Wearing all black, the assailant put a knife to Skyler's throat. The camera's field of view only included the kidnapper's waist and torso. His face was obscured. The blade glimmered in the thug's gloved hand. The camera was on a tripod, and they still appeared to be on the boat.

Skyler screamed and cried through the duct tape, but her pleas had no effect. No one was coming to save her, and she'd get no sympathy from her captors.

The kidnapper sliced the blade across her neck, spewing a geyser of crimson. It looked like a scene from a horror movie.

Skyler fell out of frame.

The blade was slick with blood.

The kidnapper wiped the residue on his pants.

Skyler's bodyguard, Maverick, was forced into the frame and onto his knees.

The kidnapper drew a pistol and put two bullets into his back.

Maverick tumbled forward out of frame.

Owen shrieked in horror.

His throat tightened, and the shriek turned into a squeak. His knees went weak, and he wobbled. The phone slipped from his grasp as his body went numb.

I caught him before he fell to the deck.

JD and I helped Owen to the settee, and his bodyguards looked on, stunned.

I picked up his phone from the deck and sent the video clip to my phone. From there, I forwarded it to Isabella to see if she could pull any metadata, but I wasn't hopeful.

Owen's world had been turned upside down. His skin was a pale, sickly color and misting with sweat. "I think I'm going to be sick."

He stood up, staggered to the gunwale, and did his business over the edge. It plopped into the water below.

Jordan got him a washcloth to clean up with, and we helped him back to the settee. Owen was in a haze. The words dribbled from his mouth, "I need to lie down."

We helped him to his master stateroom.

Owen moaned and sobbed. I didn't know the guy, but it was hard to see him in so much pain.

He groaned and whimpered, curling on his bed in the fetal position. We gave him some privacy, and Mr. Granite said he would look after his boss.

I assured him that we would continue to look for the kidnappers and bring them to justice. I said to Jordan, "Let Owen know we are not giving up."

Jordan nodded.

We showed ourselves off the boat and hustled down the dock to the parking lot.

"That was brutal," JD muttered along the way.

"Guess they didn't want any witnesses."

"I guess. But that was pouring salt in a wound."

"Maybe this was personal," I said. "Maybe they never had any intention of letting her go."

I called the sheriff and let him know that we were now dealing with a homicide investigation. Though, without bodies, it would be difficult to convict anyone.

We drove from Sandpiper Point to Mangrove Bay and looked for Oakley Sherman's boat, the *Oakster*. It was an older 32' sailboat that looked in pretty decent shape. It wouldn't be sailing around the world anytime soon, but it was cheap and functional.

We boarded the boat and banged on the hatch.

There was no response.

I banged another heavy fist, but there was no reply.

"Think he's at the club?" JD asked.

"I suspect Bert is short on DJs right about now."

We left Mangrove Bay and took the van to the Pussycat Palace. The traffic coming into town was insane. An endless river of metal. With windows down, music pumped and drifted through the air. Passengers bobbed their heads with the beat, laughed, and made the most of the journey. The party was just beginning, and eager faces anticipated the adventure that lay ahead.

We turned in and found a place to park. There was a pretty decent crowd. Music spilled out of the club and drifted across the lot. Denver wasn't working the door today. I figured he was on night shift only.

I flashed my badge to the day shift bouncer as we pushed into the dim establishment. I glanced around but didn't see Bert.

We made our way across the floor to the DJ booth. An eye-catching redhead strutted her stuff on stage, peeling away frilly garments, letting her glorious bounty spring free.

I recognized Oakley from the DMV photo Denise had sent me. He was a skinny guy with angular features, brooding brown eyes, and short hair that was long on top and dyed blue. He had a fresh baby face and couldn't have been more than 22 or 23. He bobbed up and down with the beat of the music.

I flashed my badge. "You Oakley Sherman?"

He shouted over the music. "Yeah, why?"

His concerned eyes flicked between the two of us.

"We just have some routine questions for you."

"I'm guessing this is about Shane?"

I nodded.

He gestured for us to hang on. The song was coming to an end. He leaned into the microphone. "Let's give it up for Charity."

There were hoots and hollers and a few whistles.

He spun up another tune, and another voluptuous blonde took the stage as Charity strutted away. "Let's give a warm welcome for Cassie!"

Oakley returned his attention to us.

"Can you tell me where you were last night?" I asked.

"You mean during the shooting?"

I nodded.

"I was with a friend. We went out to a few bars."

"Bars close at two. Where were you between two and three?"

"Leaving the bar and going home."

"Who's this friend?"

"Am I a suspect?"

"You *did* have a physical altercation with the deceased. You made threatening statements."

His face crinkled, then he shook his head dismissively. "Big deal. I didn't kill the guy."

"It's my understanding there was a little something between you and Honey."

His face tensed. "Just because I didn't like the guy doesn't mean I killed him." He frowned. "And Honey's married."

"That doesn't seem to affect her dating life."

"Talk to Ian. He'll tell you I was with him all evening."

"What kind of car do you drive?"

"A GS 87."

"What color?"

"Red."

It was a sporty two-door import.

"I'm guessing you'll take over Shane's shifts."

"Some of them. Bert's splitting them up between me and Gates. At least until Bert hires someone else."

"You still have a crush on Honey?"

He looked annoyed. "Is that any of your business?"

I shrugged.

"She made her choice abundantly clear. I try not to obsess over things I can't have."

"Now that her choice isn't around anymore..."

He clenched his jaw again. "Listen, I told you. I didn't kill Shane. Quit harassing me."

"What's your friend's name?"

"Ian Wolf," Oakley said. "Talk to him. He'll tell you everything you want to know."

16

"Yeah, we hit a couple bars and ended up at Bumper," Ian said. "We stayed there till two."

"What did you do after that?" I asked.

Ian was 29 and had a few prison tats. His arms were sleeved, and a few tattoos extended beyond his collar to his neck. His dark hair was trimmed into a thick mohawk.

According to the DMV, there was a black charger registered in his name.

He lived in the *Gannet Court* apartments on Community Street. It was a modest complex a few blocks from the beach, with a lot of parking and no security gate. A few palm trees dotted the property, and the grounds were well-maintained.

"I dropped Oakley off at the marina," Ian said.

"You didn't stop by the Pussycat Palace?"

"No."

"You sure about that?"

He glared at me. "Positive."

"You own a gun?"

"No. I don't believe in violence," he deadpanned.

I stifled a chuckle.

I didn't believe that for one second. He looked like a hardcore dude. He had priors for assault, possession of a controlled substance, and theft. He'd done a nickel in state prison.

"Mind if we search your car?"

His brow knitted. "Why do you want to search my car?"

"A witness could have mistaken a Charger for a Camaro."

"I told you, we didn't go by the Palace last night. And if we did, you think I'd be stupid enough to leave evidence in my car?"

He may not have been a Nobel laureate, but he knew how to handle himself on the street.

Since there were no shell casings found on the scene, I figured there might be a few in the footwell of whatever vehicle was used to carry out the attack. You'd think the shooter would be smart enough to clean the car afterward, but it was worth looking.

"If you can get a warrant, I'll let you search my car," he said in a condescending tone, almost baby-talking us. "Until then, you're just going to have to fuck off. Sorry about that."

He had a smug smile that made you want to erase it with your fist.

"We may be back," I said.

We left his apartment and walked across the lot to the Wild Fury van.

I dialed Isabella and asked her to track Oakley's and Ian's phones. I knew I was getting in deep with favors.

Her fingers danced across the keys. After a few moments of sifting through the data, she said, "Both of those phones dropped off the grid at a little after 2 AM."

"That's odd," I said in a sarcastic voice.

"Maybe they were out partying at Bumper and decided to swing by the Palace and take care of a troublesome DJ."

"It would be a helluva coincidence for both batteries to die at the same time."

I thanked her for the info and ended the call.

We searched the parking lot for Ian's Charger. I photographed the tire tread and took pictures of the vehicle. JD and I peered through the windows, but I didn't see any shell casings in the footwells.

I texted the images to Brenda to see if they matched up with the tire marks in the parking lot of the strip club.

We left the apartment complex and headed to Oyster Avenue to grab lunch.

I got a call from a guy named Derek Wise along the way. "I spoke with someone at the department. They said to talk to you."

"What can I do for you?"

"I know who killed Shane."

17

"I don't know if Desiree pulled the trigger," Derek said. "But she's behind this. I know it."

"Got any proof?" I asked.

"She's been trying to get rid of him for a while. Shane was paranoid about that. He told me he felt like he was being followed around for the last couple weeks. They weren't getting along, and she's dating that fucking loser."

"Theo?"

"Yeah."

"I'll ask again. You got any proof?"

"What more proof do you need?"

"A smoking gun would be nice."

"Okay, I can't prove it. But I'm telling you, Desiree is behind this. Look, Shane was my best friend. He kept saying he had a bad feeling. You know when you get that feeling, and you just can't explain it. It's like he knew he was gonna die. The things he said. The way he talked. It's so clear to me in hindsight."

"You know Knox Weaver?"

"That's the guy Desiree shot, right?"

"Yeah."

"I didn't really know him. I think I met him once or twice. He came into the club on occasion."

"Did you go to high school with Shane?"

"No. I moved down here a couple years ago."

"Desiree seems to think Shane hired Knox to kill her."

Derek hesitated for a moment. "If he did, it was only because he was afraid for his own life."

"That doesn't make it justifiable."

"Shane didn't hire Knox. He would have said something to me. We were tight."

"So, Knox just picked Shane's house to rob at random," I snarked.

Derek hesitated again. "I don't think it was random."

"You think he was after something specific?"

There was another long pause. "I don't know how much I should say."

"That sounds like something I should hear."

Derek sighed. "There were a lot of people that wanted to rip Shane off."

"Why is that? Was he flashy? Did he keep a lot of cash at the house?"

The line was silent.

"Why don't you tell me what's going on? It's not like your friend's going to get in trouble. He's already dead."

"Shane was dealing," Derek said. "So, yeah. He had a lot of cash and product at the house. Knox was a cokehead. I'm sure he thought he could rip Shane off and get away with it."

"Do you know where Shane was getting his supply?"

"No. That was Shane's deal. I didn't get involved with that."

"Did he owe anybody money?"

"Not that I know of."

"Was he getting his product on consignment, or was he paying cash up front?"

"I don't know. Like I said, I didn't want to get involved in that."

I think Derek knew more than he was saying, but that's all I could get out of him at the moment. "Call me if you think of anything else that might be helpful."

"I will. But you need to look into Desiree."

"Trust me. We will."

I ended the call and slipped the phone back into my pocket.

We found a place to park a few blocks from Oyster Avenue. We walked to the strip and weaved through the tourists.

The *Seashore Market* was packed, and it took forever to get a table. I was beginning to think we should avoid mainstream restaurants for the next few weeks as the horde of Spring Breakers descended upon the island.

We finally got seated in a booth by the window. Throngs of college students drifted up and down the sidewalk, some of them tacking like ships into the wind. Beer for breakfast was on the menu for most revelers. Some of them wouldn't make it to the afternoon without passing out. It was that time of year again.

We perused the menu, and JD ordered the Honey Butter Lobster Biscuits. I went with the wood-fired Lobster Pizza.

The kitchen was slow to get the food out. Everybody seemed like they were in the weeds.

My phone buzzed with a call from Denise. "I've got some interesting news about Lauren Alexander. If there was any question about this being an accident, that's been put to rest."

18

"There were small remote detonators on the brake lines and the fuel line," Denise said.

I lifted a surprised brow. "That sounds intentional."

"I'd say so."

"What do we know about the remote devices?"

"They were used to trigger det cord wrapped around the lines. Cut them clean. This is where it gets interesting. The devices were manufactured by ARMG Unlimited."

"This is starting to sound like a conspiracy."

"I agree."

"Thanks for the heads up."

"No problem. Be careful out there."

I ended the call, and the waitress clinked our entrées on the table a moment later. JD and I chowed down, then headed to ARMG Unlimited to have a word with the CEO, Noah Benson.

The company was located on the fourth floor of the Devlin-Morris building. It was on the northeast side of the island, a block from the beach. We pulled into the parking lot and climbed the steps to the main entrance. Sunlight flowed into the atrium from skylights. We took a small footbridge over a Koi pond to the glass elevator that vaulted us up to the fourth floor.

Floor-to-ceiling glass doors partitioned the main entrance to ARMG Unlimited. We stepped inside and were greeted by a receptionist behind a desk. The office was sleek and modern. A large flatscreen display on the wall looped a trailer of the company's various products. They had a hand in everything.

I flashed my badge to the receptionist and smiled.

She looked concerned.

"We are investigating the death of Lauren Alexander and Dylan Reynolds."

She sighed, slumping over the desk. Her sad eyebrows knitted, and she frowned. "It's just terrible. Here one minute, gone the next."

"Is Noah Benson available?"

"He's extremely busy, but let me buzz him and see if he has a moment to speak with you."

She dialed an extension. "Mr. Benson, there are two deputies here to see you. They're inquiring about Lauren and Dylan." She listened intently for a moment. "Okay. I'll tell them."

She ended the call and looked up at me with a smile. She had a nice smile.

"He'll be with you momentarily," she said. "Please, make yourself at home." She motioned to the white mid-century modern chairs and sofa. "Can I get you anything to drink? Water, tea, coffee?"

"No, thank you," I said.

We took a seat, and JD flipped through a car magazine. Since his Porsche had been set ablaze, he was in the market.

I watched the flatscreen display as the company's show-reel played. They did everything from aerospace to home security. They developed specialty compounds for all sorts of industries, including the military. The announcer uttered the company's tagline, "Advance Research and Materials Group is building a better, safer world, one product at a time."

A young brunette in a tight cream dress strutted into the waiting area, her high heels clacking against the tile. "Deputies, Mr. Benson will see you now."

I stood up and smiled at the receptionist as we passed.

The delightful brunette introduced herself as "Jessica, Mr. Benson's assistant." She led us down a hallway to Noah's office. JD and I couldn't help but notice the enticing sway of her hips.

She motioned us into Noah's office, and he stood up from behind his desk and greeted us with a smile.

Jessica left.

I wouldn't have minded if she had stayed.

We both shook hands with Noah and made introductions. He offered us a seat in the two leather chairs across from his glass desk. Behind him, floor-to-ceiling windows offered a nice view of the ocean, whitecaps frothing in the distance, the sun sparkling the water.

His office was sleek and minimal. A thin, all-in-one desktop sat on his desk. There were pictures of himself with heads of state, military officers, and several photos of him in the field with various airplanes, and even in the trenches with the grunts. He was smiling in every picture.

Noah was in his mid-40s with wavy brown hair, a square jaw, and a dimple in his chin. He had narrow brown eyes and carried himself with the unflappable confidence and self-congratulatory demeanor of a successful entrepreneur.

He frowned and shook his head. "Such a tragic loss. From what I understand, there is talk that this wasn't just an accident."

"We have reason to believe either Lauren or Dylan were targeted," I said. "Perhaps both."

"Why do you think that?"

"Well, usually in accidents like this, we don't see remote detonators and explosives on fuel and brake lines."

His eyes rounded. "That is concerning," he said in an understated tone.

"I would agree. Even more concerning, the devices used were manufactured by your company."

His jaw dropped.

I gave him the details.

His face tensed with confusion. "I don't understand. These types of products are strictly regulated."

"Who would have access to the devices?"

"Can you tell me the make and model number?"

I showed him images on my phone of fragments that Denise had texted me.

Noah studied them carefully. "That's one of ours, alright. Looks like a DetCon 245T." He frowned and shook his head. "I'm more than happy to work with your forensic team to track down the lot number and identify where these came from and who had access."

"We appreciate that."

"Do you have any leads at this time?"

"That's what we're hoping you can help us with."

"Like I said, I will do whatever I can. Lauren and Dylan were both valued employees. This is a great loss for our organization."

"Were you aware that the two were having an affair?"

He sucked in a tense breath. "We frown on that kind of thing here. But I think it was obvious to anyone who spent any time around the two. There was something going on, no doubt. There was a certain chemistry between them. They were both great employees. They both had high sales numbers. I tend to overlook a lot of things if an individual is performing well. At the end of the day, we're here to make money. I'm not the morality police."

"Do you know Lauren's husband?"

"I met him a few times. Company gatherings, Christmas parties, etc. Nice guy. Older gentleman. I wasn't sure how much they had in common. Quite frankly, it didn't surprise me when she took an interest in Dylan. He was, by all standards, handsome and very charming. Did well with the ladies. Lauren certainly wasn't the first woman to fall under his spell," he said with a smirk.

"Did either have any enemies within the company?" I asked.

"As I mentioned, they were both top performers. You don't get to the number one slot without ruffling a few feathers. Sales is a competitive business. And both were very aggressive.

"Whose feathers did they ruffle?"

19

Noah thought for a moment. "I don't want to throw anybody under the bus, but Timothy and Dylan butted heads from time to time. I do remember words were exchanged at the Christmas party." He dismissed the notion. "But we're talking premeditated murder here. That goes a little beyond interoffice rivalries."

"What was the issue between them?" I asked.

Noah took a deep breath and sighed. "I guess this reflects on me and my lack of enforcing office policies. Timothy had a massive crush on Lauren. He made a few attempts and was shut down. Then, when she connected with Dylan, there was instant jealousy."

"Did the two ever get into a physical altercation?"

"Not that I'm aware of. I think there were some pretty heated exchanges between them around the water cooler. It all came to a head at the party. There was some shoving, but it was broken up quickly. I can't imagine that Timothy would sabotage Lauren's vehicle and kill them both. That just seems ridiculous to me."

"Never underestimate the power of love," JD said with a slightly sardonic tone.

"I guess anything is possible."

"Was Lauren's husband at the Christmas party?" I asked.

"Yes, he was."

"What did he think about two other men fighting over his wife?"

"I don't think he was aware of the nature of the conflict."

"Any other office rivalries that we should know about?"

Noah contemplated the question for a moment. "I mean, I guess you could say there was a little animosity between Marissa and Lauren. Like I said, it's a competitive business. Lauren had the largest territory of any salesperson here. Quite often, she tended to ignore boundaries. At the end of the day, a sale is a sale." He paused. "And there may be a few other factors at play."

"Such as?"

Noah leaned in and whispered. "Everyone's entitled to their own beliefs, but Marissa is very religious. Though I think she overlooked the part about judgment. She thought Lauren's behavior with Dylan was reprehensible and unbecoming. She brought it to my attention on numerous occasions. She suggested that employees having extramarital affairs reflected poorly on the values of the company." He raised his hands innocently. "I'm not condoning affairs, mind you. But it's really none of my business. If it would have affected their performance, I would have cracked down." He paused, then admitted, "It did make it a little awkward knowing what was going on between them and then having to talk to Lauren's husband and act like everything was fine."

"He knew," I said.

Noah lifted a surprised brow, then sighed. "Well, everybody's gotta decide what they're willing to tolerate. Infidelity is a dealbreaker for some. For others, it's an unpleasant reality of their relationship. A cost of doing business."

"We'd like to have a word with both of them," I said.

"Certainly. You can talk in the conference room, if you'd like a little privacy."

"That would be great."

"I'll have Jessica escort you. Who do you want to talk to first?"

20

Timothy was a skinny guy with a large forehead, wavy brown hair, and big nervous eyes. Despite being in his late 20s, he still had a baby face. He lacked the charisma, charm, and handsome looks of Dylan Reynolds. Timothy had been losing out to guys like Dylan his whole life. That kind of resentment compounds over time. He didn't look like the kind of guy who confronted situations head-on. His resentment must have been festering by the time he exploded at the Christmas party. He struck me as the shy guy who could just snap one day. Walk into the office with a semi-automatic rifle and take everyone out. Friends and colleagues would say how nice and reserved he was. How he just went mad.

Of course, that was just a first impression.

"You wanted to see me?" Timothy said as he stepped into the conference room.

I offered him a seat, and he slid into the leather chair across from us. I flashed my badge and made introductions.

"We just have some routine questions for you," I said, hoping to disarm him.

"Sure, anything I can do to help."

"Can you tell me where you were the evening that Lauren and Dylan were killed?"

His face wrinkled, and he stammered, "Yeah. I was out with a friend at Turtles for happy hour. Then we hit Mutiny, then Red November, if I recall."

"I'll need your friend's name and contact information."

"Sure. His name is Gareth. Gareth Moore. What does that have to do with anything?"

I showed him a picture of the detonator fragments. He studied the images on my phone.

"You know what those are?"

"Not really."

"It's a remote detonation device triggered over a cellular network. It's manufactured by ARMG."

His confused gaze flicked from the images to me. "What does that have to do with me?"

"Do you have access to the devices?"

"No."

"But you sell them, right?"

"I sell a lot of products. When we do demonstrations for the military or law enforcement, we always have our technical team bring weapons and demonstrate them. It's tightly controlled and regulated. Very rarely do we handle items of that nature, unless it's a dummy prototype to show the client." He paused. "I'm still having a hard time following where this is going."

"Those devices were found under Lauren's car."

His eyes rounded. "So, she was murdered?"

"We believe so, yes."

There was a genuine look of surprise and confusion on his face.

"What kind of car do you drive?" I asked.

"A black Navigator."

I exchanged a glance with JD. The DOT footage of the incident was of poor quality. We were unable to determine the exact make and model of the assailant's vehicle.

"It's my understanding that Dylan wasn't your favorite person," I said.

Timothy stared at me for a moment and swallowed hard. "We weren't the best of friends."

"You were jealous of Dylan's relationship with Lauren."

His face twisted. "No. I wasn't jealous."

"You had asked Lauren out previously."

He shook his head. "No."

"You never asked her out for drinks?" My tone was skeptical and accusatory.

"Not in the way you're thinking. I suggested we grab drinks as friends."

"Friends?"

He nodded.

"You never had a romantic interest in Lauren."

He hesitated. "I mean, she was a beautiful woman. I think every man that saw her felt something."

"What did you feel?"

"I felt like she was an attractive woman, and I wanted to spend more time with her."

"As friends," I snarked.

"Yes, as friends. She was married. I would never do anything inappropriate with a married woman."

I didn't buy it for a second. Lauren was a woman who could make most men compromise their values. One's moral resolve tends to diminish as blood flow moves south, feeding the little brain.

"How did you feel when you found out Lauren was sleeping with Dylan?"

Timothy's jaw flexed, and his cheeks reddened. It was an involuntary response, and it told me exactly how he felt. "I felt... surprised. I didn't think Dylan was her type. He was too... shallow for her."

"She deserved better."

"Much."

"She deserved someone like you."

"I think I could have given her everything she needed," he said with confidence.

"If she weren't married."

"Correct. If she weren't married."

"So, you were perfectly happy just being friends?"

"I didn't have the option to be anything else."

"Did that make you angry?"

"It's foolish to get angry about things you can't change," Timothy said. "It is what it is. It's like getting angry because the sky is blue."

"But you asked her out for drinks, and she turned you down."

"I think she misunderstood my intentions."

"Usually when a guy asks a woman out for drinks, his intentions are pretty clear."

"I'm not your average guy."

"You're special," I said, patronizing him.

"I'm sure you think you're special too, deputy. Look, I didn't sabotage Lauren's car because she turned me down. I wasn't jealous of Dylan. There are a lot better men to be jealous of. Dylan was a loser. Lauren would have figured that out in time."

He paused for a long moment, his eyes darting between the two of us.

"If that's all, I need to get back to work," he said.

I slid my card across the table. "If you can think of anything else helpful, let me know."

He looked at the card but didn't take it. Timothy climbed from his chair and stepped out of the conference room.

I grabbed the phone on the desk, dialed Noah's extension, and told him we were ready to speak with Marissa.

"I'll send her right in."

I hung up the phone.

JD muttered, "I'm not so sure about that kid."

"I'm certainly not ruling him out."

Marissa entered the conference room a few moments later. I offered her a chair.

She was a sweet, wholesome blonde with curly golden hair, sleepy blue eyes, and classic features. She looked like she stepped out of a Norman Rockwell painting. Despite her pious demeanor, sinful temptations lay hidden under that dress. It was tight enough to ignite a few lustful desires.

"This is Deputy Donovan, and I'm Deputy Wild. How's your day going?"

She took a seat across the table from us. "Could be better. Could be worse. Is it true you think Lauren and Dylan were murdered?"

I nodded.

"Well, I hate to speak ill of the dead, but she wasn't living right. This doesn't surprise me. Live by the sword, die by the sword."

"Did she live by the sword?"

"Swords, really," she snarked. "One wasn't enough." There was utter disdain in her voice.

"It's clear you didn't approve of her lifestyle choices."

"People are free to do whatever they want. But actions have consequences."

"You think she deserved to die?"

"It's not for me to judge. Just merely making an observation."

I showed her the pictures of the detonator fragments. "Do you know what those are?"

She surveyed the images carefully. "Is this a competency test?"

"I don't think so."

"Well, those appear to be fragments of a DetCon 245T. It's a highly specialized remote detonator that is made exclusively for military purposes. Where were those photos taken?"

"The fragments were recovered from Lauren's vehicle."

Marissa arched a curious eyebrow. She looked almost amused. "Now that's interesting, indeed."

"Why would you say that?"

"Well, that device is under strict control. And we've shipped limited quantities. Right now, I think there are only a few special forces units that have access to those devices." She smiled. "And I put that deal together."

"You must be a hell of a salesperson."

She smiled. "We have good products. They sell themselves. But I take care of our customers. It's unfortunate my contributions haven't been fully recognized."

"You feel overshadowed by Lauren."

"I'm not standing in her shadow anymore, now am I?"

"Sounds like a motive for murder," I said.

That hung there for a moment.

21

Marissa's blue eyes narrowed at me. "I didn't approve of Lauren's behavior. That's no secret. But as I said, it's not for me to judge. Only God can do that."

"Where were you the night of the accident?" I asked.

"I was at home."

"Alone?"

"No. Not alone. I was with Skipper and Mr. Cuddles."

"Your cats?"

"I like to think of them as my children."

"I don't suppose they're able to confirm your alibi."

"Are you accusing me of something?"

"Not at the moment."

"While I can appreciate your thoroughness, I can assure you, I did not have a hand in that woman's demise. I take no joy in her passing," she said in a tone that attempted to be sincere but revealed her hidden glee. "Maybe if she would have gotten right with the Lord, this kind of thing would never have happened."

"What about Dylan?"

She scoffed. "I think that boy was beyond salvation. The devil comes not as evil but disguised as everything you've ever wanted."

"Did you want Dylan Reynolds?"

She laughed as if the notion was preposterous. But I suspected otherwise. "I have more self respect than to pine for a man like Dylan."

"Did you two ever date?"

"Heavens no."

"What kind of car do you drive?" I asked.

"A Miata. Why?"

"Just curious."

"You think I ran her off the road and rigged the lines on her car to blow, using devices that could be tracked back to me, all because I was jealous?"

"The thought had occurred to me."

"Do I look stupid to you, Deputy Wild?"

"Not particularly."

"I can assure you, I'm not stupid. If I was going to kill that wretched woman, I would have done it in a much more sophisticated way." She held her nose high. "But that is neither here nor there. This may come as a shock to you, but murder is generally frowned upon in the eyes of the Lord."

"Sadly, that doesn't seem to slow many people down."

She gave a sympathetic sigh. "Life seems to have little value anymore."

"Out of curiosity, how do you reconcile selling weapons of mass destruction with your spiritual beliefs?" I was genuinely curious.

She smiled. "That's a great question. I'm so glad you asked. I believe my work empowers the righteous to do their job. Without law and order, there would be chaos. As a company, we are merely providing the necessary equipment and technology to maintain that order. I sleep well at night. How about you?"

22

I slept pretty well at night, actually. JD and I were trying to do the right thing, and I was trying to only kill people when absolutely necessary. There were times when I wanted to break that rule, but I'd been playing things by the book. I had been given a second chance at life, and I was trying to make the most of it.

I gave Marissa a card. She left the conference room, and we said a few words to Noah before leaving ARMG. I texted Isabella as we drove back toward Diver Down and asked her to track Marissa's and Timothy's cell phones the night of the accident.

"Marissa is a piece of work," JD said.

"I don't see her crawling underneath Lauren's car and rigging the lines to blow," I said.

"You never know. She seems smart, resourceful, and opinionated."

"And potentially homicidal. Sounds like your kind of woman."

JD grinned. "She might be able to make me repent."

I laughed, then dialed Gareth Moore. I put the call on speaker so JD could hear.

Gareth answered after a few rings, and I introduced myself. "I'm investigating the death of Lauren Alexander and Dylan Reynolds. I'm hoping you can answer a few questions for me."

"I don't really know those people."

"You know Timothy, don't you?"

"Yeah."

"Did he mention his coworkers were killed?"

"Yeah. He said something about it."

"Can you tell me where you were the evening Lauren and Dylan died?"

"We hung out at Turtles and hit a few bars."

"When did you part company that evening?"

"It was probably around midnight."

"You sure about that?"

He hesitated. "Yeah. I'm positive."

"You could be charged with obstruction of justice if I catch you lying."

"I'm not lying!"

"Who drove?"

"I met him at Turtles. I don't know if he drove or cabbed it."

"What kind of car do you drive?"

"A Mercedes G-Wagon."

"You must do well for yourself," I said. The model had been insanely marked up for a while.

"I do ok."

"What color?"

"Jet black metallic."

I exchanged a glance with JD. The black SUV that ran Lauren off the road didn't look like a G-Wagon, but the footage wasn't that great.

My phone buzzed with a call from Denise. I told Gareth I'd be in touch, then clicked over.

"Hey, you've got a problem," Denise said.

"What is it now?"

"Your client, Owen. He's not your client anymore."

My brow knitted. "What do you mean?"

"You should turn on the news."

"What happened?"

"He decided to tie an anchor around his waist and jump off his yacht while they were at sea. A neighboring boat happened to catch the whole thing on video. Paris has been looping it as a breaking news segment every 15 minutes."

I cringed. "Has the body been recovered?"

"Dive team is looking now. Daniels wants you on the scene ASAP."

"Owen was pretty broken up about the death of his girlfriend," I said. "I can't say this comes as a shock. Poor guy."

I thanked her for the update, and we hustled back to the marina. JD parked the van, and we raced down the dock to the wake boat, hopped in, and cast off the lines. JD took the helm and idled us past the breakwater. He brought the boat on plane, and the engines howled. The craft carved through the teal swells. Mists of saltwater sprayed.

Denise had texted me the sheriff's current location, and it didn't take long to arrive at the scene.

Several Coast Guard and county patrol boats were in the water. Divers surfaced with Owen's body, and deputies helped pull the remains onto a Defender class patrol boat.

Owen had been in the water for quite some time. There was no reviving him.

Jack frowned. "Seemed like a decent kid. He was willing to give up everything for the woman he loved. Gotta admire that. These days, you're lucky to get a return phone call."

JD navigated the wake boat to the swim platform of Owen's superyacht. We tied off and boarded the boat. Owen's security staff looked on from the aft deck, and we climbed the molded-in steps to join them.

"What happened?" I asked.

Mr. Granite looked distraught. "I thought Owen had calmed down a little," Jordan said. "I left him alone in his stateroom to give him some privacy. He told me to have the captain take us out to sea. He needed to clear his head. We left the marina and were heading toward Angelfish Island. We planned on looping around and coming back to Coconut Key unless instructed otherwise. We'd been underway for a little while when I went to check on Owen. I looked in his stateroom, and he was gone. I thought maybe he'd gotten up and gone into the galley. He wasn't there. Leo and I searched the boat, but we couldn't find him anywhere. I started to get worried. I'd never seen Owen so distraught. I mean, you saw him. The guy was crushed. We radioed the Coast Guard and notified them that we had a man overboard. Turns out someone had seen Owen go over and had already contacted them. They had him on video, and they didn't even stop to help. Can you believe it?"

I could believe anything.

Jordan's face reddened, and his jaw flexed. His eyes grew slick. "They sure didn't waste any time selling the clip to the news channels."

I could tell Jordan liked Owen. It was more than just a job.

"Whoever called in gave their approximate location when they saw Owen go overboard. The Coast Guard told us, so we circled back and met up with the sheriff's deputies and the Coast Guard." Jordan hung his head. "I owe that guy everything. He gave me a job when I had nothing. He treated us well. Paid us more than what we would have made elsewhere. Treated us with respect. I've worked for rich assholes that didn't give two shits about their employees. Owen was different."

Leo gave us his version of events. His recollection mirrored Jordan's statement.

I searched the Internet for the clip. It was on every news website and had already gone viral.

JD hovered nearby as we watched the video on my phone.

Owen stood on the swim platform, holding a Danforth anchor. He stepped off, plunged into the water with a small splash, and disappeared into the abyss.

This incident was open and shut. There was clearly no foul play involved.

Owen was a likable guy with a friendly demeanor. Understandably high-strung, but likable. I couldn't help but feel terrible about the situation.

We left the superyacht and boarded the wake boat. I cast off the lines, and we pulled alongside the sheriff's patrol boat and exchanged a few brief words before heading back to Coconut Key. The mood was somber. We both felt like we had failed Owen.

We stopped by the station, filled out reports, then cruised back to Diver Down. JD navigated the wake boat into the slip, and I tied off. I took Buddy out for a quick walk, then we stopped in the bar to chat with Teagan.

Paris Delaney was still on air, conversing with the in-studio news anchor about Owen Patterson. "In the wake of the CEO's death, shocking allegations have come to light…"

23

"Sources inside the crypto exchange claim the company is bankrupt," Paris said. "In what is being described as a massive Ponzi scheme, the firm sold tokens to investors, which were then used as collateral to purchase other assets. With the recent kidnapping of model and influencer Skyler Graham, founder and CEO Owen Patterson used these fraudulent funds to pay her ransom. Sadly, Skyler, her bodyguard Maverick Jones, and Patterson are all deceased."

"What a stunning turn of events," the desk anchor said.

"I recently spoke with several investors. Here's what one, who agreed to speak on camera, had to say.

The segment cut to an interview with a man in his early 50s. His hair was thinning on top, and he was starting to gray on the sides. He had a trimmed beard, and a distraught look tensed his face. "I lost everything. I put my entire life savings into that exchange and those tokens. My nephew had made a killing in crypto and convinced me to start investing in the stuff. At first, the returns were great. Hell, there were all kinds of celebrity endorsements. But I bought a token that was worthless. This is unconscionable. Somebody needs to go to jail."

The segment cut back to Paris. "Just heartbreaking. I spoke with several more investors, all with similar stories. I'm sure we'll be sifting through the debris of this scandal for quite some time. I'm Paris Delaney, and you heard it from me first."

"Thank you, Paris," the news anchor said.

"Maybe Owen wasn't such a nice guy after all," JD said.

"He was desperate," I said. "Desperate people do desperate things."

"He was defrauding his customers long before this scenario."

"Do you have any leads on the kidnappers?" Teagan asked.

I shook my head.

"So, this guy defrauds investors, uses the money to pay the ransom, and the kidnappers get off scot-free?"

"Not if we have anything to say about it."

We hung out, had a drink, then headed to band practice. JD drove the van to the warehouse district and pulled into the lot.

The usual group of miscreants with jet-black hair and painted fingernails hung out in front of the entrance, wearing skinny jeans, smoking cigarettes, and drinking beer. There were high-fives all around as we stepped inside the warehouse and into the dim hallway that smelled of beer and illicit herb. We made our way to the rehearsal space, and JD unlocked the door. We pushed into the small room.

The guys in the band hadn't arrived yet.

There was a small note on the floor that someone had shoved under the door. Jack almost stepped on it before noticing it. He snatched it up, unfolded the paper, and read the note.

A scowl tensed his face, then he handed it to me. "What do you make of that?"

I read the note. "I think whoever wrote this doesn't like the band?"

"They clearly have no taste," JD said. "Should we take it seriously?"

"I think we should take all threats seriously."

JD shrugged it off. "It's a sign of success. You're nobody until somebody hates you."

"I'll have the lab run an analysis on this. Maybe they can pull a print or determine the type of paper and where it came from. This guy clearly isn't in his right mind."

The rumble of neighboring bands practicing filtered through the walls—booming bass drums, grinding guitars, and aggressive vocals. Some of it sounded good. Some of it not so much.

I plugged into Crash's bass rig and noodled around while we waited. I'd been practicing for a while and wasn't half bad by now.

When the guys arrived, I told them about the death threat and let them read the note.

"Tell that punk to bring it," Dizzy spouted. "We'll fuck him up."

The guys could talk a good game, but they were skinny rockers. Worthless in a bar fight. Bravado does little good against a knife, a gun, or a pipe bomb.

They ran through the set and fine-tuned a new song. A few regular groupies showed up for a free show, but most of the usual crowd was occupied with the festivities on Oyster Avenue.

I was more cautious about who we let into the practice space. Playing live shows in crowded spaces was a security nightmare. If somebody really wanted to get to the band, it wouldn't be hard.

After practice, JD took the guys to dinner, then we hit our usual haunt, *Tide Pool*. We hung out by the outdoor pool, and JD bought a round of drinks for the guys.

The place was packed. You could barely move, slithering between bodies, which wasn't always a bad thing. There were plenty of beauties in teeny bikinis, the fabric made translucent by the water. The smell of chlorine and strawberry daiquiris filled the air. Chill music pumped from speakers.

The influx of tourists always changed the dynamic on the island for a few weeks. All of our usual spots were overrun. It was standing room only. There was no place to grab a seat, so we loitered around the pool, mixing and mingling.

We were into the second round when JD's eyes narrowed at someone across the pool. "I'll be damned. Would you look at that?"

He pointed across the water.

Pretty people frolicked in the pool, sloshing and splashing, batting a beach ball around. I searched the crowd of faces but didn't see anyone notable.

"I could have sworn I just saw Veronica or whatever the hell her name is."

I surveyed the crowd but still didn't see JD's stalker.

"It was her. I'm sure of it."

"Well, she's gone now."

"She dyed her hair," he said. "She's a blonde now."

"When was the last time you had your vision checked?"

Jack scowled at me.

"I'm telling you, it was her!"

"Why would she come back here? There's a warrant out for her arrest. I'd hightail it out of here and never come back."

JD puffed up with pride. "Maybe I'm irresistible. She came back for one more glimpse."

I rolled my eyes.

"I'm going to get to the bottom of this. I'll be right back." He pushed through the crowd, walking around the pool.

"Where are you going?" I shouted after him.

"Looking for trouble."

Veronica was trouble, indeed. She had tried to kill him once before. I began to wonder if she was behind the threatening note. Certainly possible, but it wasn't her style. She was direct. She wouldn't waste time with a note. She'd just do it.

I watched as he weaved around the patio to the other side. Jack glanced around but didn't see the elusive vixen. With a frustrated look, he pushed inside the club.

"Where is he off to?" Crash asked.

I told him.

"Man, that girl is bad news."

"You don't have to tell me."

"He's not still into her, is he?"

"That would be a whole new level of crazy for JD."

Crash shrugged.

Jack didn't always have the best judgment when it came to romantic interests. But, as they say, love is blind.

We hung out for a while, enjoying the scenery. The guys rounded up sufficient interest for a small after-party aboard the boat, and we pulled the entourage out of the bar.

Jack never did find Veronica. I think his mind was playing tricks on him. After what she did to him, I'd be a little paranoid too. I might start to see her everywhere.

The marina at Diver Down was alive with a few parties when we returned. We boarded the *Avventura* with a small group in tow. Buddy bounced and barked.

The ladies fell in love.

JD moved behind the bar in the salon and dealt out glasses of Wild Fury whiskey, creating new customers.

I took Buddy out for a late-night walk. By the time I returned to the boat, there were more than a few beauties who'd shed their attire and dipped in the Jacuzzi on the sky deck.

Not a bad way to finish out the evening. Not a bad way at all.

In the morning, I got an unexpected call. I reached a sleepy hand to the nightstand and grabbed the phone. I looked at the caller ID and swiped the screen.

"Mr. Benson," I said in a scratchy voice. "What can I do for you?"

"I hope I'm not disturbing you. I found something you should take a look at."

24

"I have access to every email sent through our system, as well as access to text messages and call logs made with company-issued phones," Noah said. "It's part of the agreement employees signed when they joined the company."

"What did you find?" I asked.

"Well, it seems that Timothy made arrangements to get some working prototypes of the detonators from our weapons division. He said he needed them for a client demonstration. The lot numbers on those devices matched the numbers that you gave me." He sighed. "I've gotta say I'm beside myself. I never would have imagined him capable of such a thing. You think you know someone."

"I'll need copies of those emails. Are you willing to come down to the station and make a sworn statement?"

"Absolutely. Whatever I can do to help."

"In the meantime, keep this between us. Just go about business as usual until we have him in custody. No need to tip him off. He may decide to run or resist if he thinks we're onto him."

"Rest assured, I will keep this conversation between us."

I told Noah I'd be down at the station in 45 minutes. He agreed to meet me there.

I pulled myself out of bed, showered, dressed, and stumbled down to the galley to fix breakfast. The boat was silent as I started brewing a pot of coffee. As usual, there were empty glasses and beer bottles scattered everywhere.

I banged on the hatch to JD's stateroom.

He groaned.

"Get your ass up," I shouted through the hatch. "We've got a break in the Lauren Alexander case."

I returned to the galley, grilled bacon, and fried eggs. JD joined me at the breakfast nook just in time to dish up. We chowed down, then headed to the station and took Noah's statement. I filled out an application for a warrant. Then we waited.

JD and I caught up with Denise at her desk. The usual bustle of activity filled the office. Deputies fielded complaints and processed perps. Fingers tapped on keyboards, and phones rang.

"You're gonna like this," Denise said with a smile.

"I like good news."

"Desiree Jeffries was picked up on a routine traffic stop. She'd been drinking and was acting a little funny. The deputy searched her vehicle and found a gram of cocaine and a 9mm pistol under the seat. Lab is running ballistics now. I'll let you know what comes of it."

"Please do."

She nodded. "Anything interesting with you boys?"

"Hopefully, we're going to make an arrest in the near future," JD said.

I caught her up to speed on the Lauren Alexander case.

We grabbed a cup of coffee while we waited and shot the breeze with Denise.

Judge Echols signed off on the warrant, and we had a tac team at Timothy's front door in no time. Suited up with bulletproof vests, extra magazines, helmets, and AR-15s, it was overkill for the situation, but better safe than sorry.

JD banged on the door and shouted, "Coconut County! We have a warrant."

Timothy lived in a gray two-story French colonial with white trim. A red brick walkway led to a small veranda with a sitting chair. The second story had a nice terrace. There was a red brick drive and a small square that I wouldn't quite call a lawn. It was home to a few ferns, shrubs, and two tall palm trees that shrouded the house.

Mendoza and Robinson had taken the rear in case he tried to escape.

Timothy opened the door before we could break it down. He gave us a quizzical look as the tactical team aimed AR-15s in his direction, the angry barrels hungry for a target. "What's going on?"

"We have a warrant to search the premises. You're under arrest for the murder of Lauren Alexander and Dylan Reynolds."

"What!?" Timothy exclaimed with a bewildered face.

"Turn around and put your hands behind your back."

"You can't arrest me. I didn't do anything!"

"We have access to all your company emails."

His face crinkled. "So?"

"Turn around and put your hands behind your back," I commanded again.

His jaw clenched, and his cheeks flushed with anger.

"Do it, now! You don't want me to think you're resisting, do you?"

He grumbled a few obscenities but complied.

JD slapped the cuffs around his wrists and ratcheted them tight. Timothy winced as the hard steel hit his boney wrists.

Jack read him his rights as he escorted him down the steps to a patrol car that waited at the curb. He stuffed him into the backseat, and we flooded into the house and rummaged through everything.

I didn't think there was anyone else in the home, but we cleared the area, room by room, then proceeded to tear the place apart, looking in drawers, cabinets, closets, etc.

The decor was stylish with light hardwoods, mint walls, and mid-century furniture. Marble countertops and brushed nickel fixtures. Timothy was an amateur photographer, and there were plenty of landscapes and street portraits matted in black frames on the walls.

In a drawer in the upstairs office, we found two of the remote detonators from the same lot as the ones used to sabotage Lauren Alexander's vehicle.

Along with the devices, we found detonation cord which can be used as a precision cutting charge. Wrapped around a fuel or brake line, the thin, flexible tube filled with pentaerythritol tetranitrate would do the job nicely.

I didn't know if it was enough circumstantial evidence to convict, but it was enough to put Timothy in the pod and give us time to sort things out. He was taken to the station, processed, printed, and put into the interrogation room.

We filled out after-action reports in the conference room. After Timothy had a sufficient amount of time to sweat, we paid him a visit.

I walked in with the detonators and det cord in an evidence bag and took a seat across the table from him. I set the devices on the table and didn't say a word.

Sweat misted his brow. Timothy's nervous eyes flicked right to them. "What are those?"

"You know damn good and well what those are."

"I know what they are. What does that have to do with me?"

"We found those in a drawer in your office."

His face crinkled. "Those aren't mine."

"They were in your possession."

"No, they weren't."

"If it's in your house, it's in your possession."

His jaw tightened, and his eyes narrowed. "I see how this is. You're setting me up. You planted those. You need a patsy to go down for this, and you think I'm your guy. Well, it's total bullshit."

"I didn't plant those items in your desk drawer. You want to tell me how they got there?"

"How should I know?"

"I guess someone snuck into your house and just magically deposited them without your knowledge."

"Anything is possible."

"Can you explain your requests for those devices from your weapons division?"

His brow knitted. "I never made a request for those."

I sneered at him in disbelief. "Stop lying. We've got access to everything. All the emails on the company server."

"Who gave those to you?" he asked, stunned.

"Does it matter?"

"Yes, it matters."

"We got them from your employer. Your employer has the right to divulge that information to law enforcement. It's in your employment contract."

The muscles in his jaw flexed, and his face reddened. The veins in his forehead bulged. "Somebody's setting me up. I didn't make those requests."

"So you're telling me that someone used your computer to make those requests?"

"I'm saying I didn't do it."

"Is your computer password-protected?"

"It is."

"Who else had access?"

"I don't know. My employer. The IT guys. Maybe a colleague saw me enter my password, or maybe someone installed a keyword sniffer. How should I know?"

He seemed sincere, but so do a lot of criminals when their back is against the wall.

"Did you find my fingerprints on those devices?"

"The lab will certainly look."

"They can look all they want. They're not going to find my prints because I never touched them. They're not mine. So run along and do your thing. When you come back, please explain to me how I'm guilty without my fingerprints on those detonators."

"You're a smart guy, Timothy. You wore gloves and wiped them down. You're not getting out of this one. There is no clever little loophole for you to slip through. Why don't you just come clean and admit what you did? Save the taxpayers the time and trouble of a trial, and maybe the state's attorney will offer you a decent deal."

"How about you go fuck yourselves? I want to speak with my lawyer."

That was the end of the interview.

I sighed and pushed away from the table. The chair screeched against the tile. I grabbed the evidence. "Suit yourself."

We walked to the door and knocked. A guard buzzed us out, and we left Timothy to contemplate his situation.

The sheriff joined us in the hallway. He'd seen the whole thing from the observation room. "No way that punk weasels out of this one. Get those to the lab ASAP. I want something tying him definitively to those devices. Skin cells, hair, whatever."

"I don't think we have to worry," JD said. "I don't care what that punk says, we caught him with his hand in the cookie jar. There's no jury around that's going to let him walk with this amount of evidence."

"I hope you're right," Daniels said. "Nice work, gentlemen." He gave Jack a pat on the back as he strolled down the hallway.

JD grinned with pride.

"Don't get ahead of yourself," I cautioned.

"Relax. He's got motive, means—"

"But not opportunity. He's got an alibi, remember?"

JD frowned. "Maybe we should have another chat with Gareth. See if his story changes."

25

Gareth lived in the Nautilus. It was a luxury high-rise with all the amenities—24-hour concierge, laundry service, gymnasium, and a rooftop pool. There was an attached marina filled with superyachts and bluewater sailboats.

We drove the van to the highrise, and JD pulled under the carport. The valet hustled to grab his door. JD hopped out, slipped him a nice wad of cash, and told him to keep the van up front.

The kid eyed the van with awe. With the Wild Fury logo emblazoned on the sides, there was no doubt who the van belonged to. The kid put two and two together as he surveyed JD. "You're Thrash, aren't you?"

It was Jack's stage name.

JD beamed with pride.

The kid high-fived him. "Rock 'n' roll!"

He hopped into the van and parked it next to a Lambo. The van was so outrageous and souped-up it didn't look out of place next to the exotic sportscar.

We stepped to the glass entry doors, and I flashed my shiny gold badge to the concierge. She buzzed us in, and we stepped inside the opulent lobby. "Good morning, deputies. What can I do for you?"

"Looking for Gareth Moore," I said.

"1722. I hope he's not in any kind of trouble."

"I hope he's not either. Do you know if he's on the premises?"

"I haven't seen him leave today."

I smiled, and she smiled back.

We strolled past the waterfall, past the baby grand piano, to the bank of elevators. JD pressed the call button, and it lit up. We watched the display tick off the floors as the elevator plummeted down to the lobby. The door slid open, and we stepped aboard.

We launched skyward, and within moments, we were stepping into the 17th hallway. We found Gareth's unit, and I put a heavy fist against the door.

The speaker in his video doorbell crackled. "What do you want?"

I flashed my badge to the lens.

"I'm Deputy Wild. We spoke the other day. I just have a few additional questions for you."

He hesitated for a moment. "I told you everything you wanted to know."

"Your friend has been arrested. I'm gonna give you one last opportunity to tell me your whereabouts the evening in question. If you don't tell me the truth, you're looking at obstruction."

The line crackled with static.

"Do you have a warrant?"

"You're making me suspicious. Just come to the door and talk to us. You tell me the truth, and I'll leave you alone."

He disconnected the call.

I looked at JD, thinking that was the end of the road.

Then I heard footsteps down the foyer.

Gareth pulled open the door a moment later and surveyed us with annoyed eyes. He was in his late 20s with short hair, brown eyes, and a trapezoidal face. He wasn't quite as nerdy as Timothy, but he wasn't GQ material either, despite his square jaw.

"You look like a smart guy," I said. "I know you're going to make the right decision. You're starting off on a good foot by opening the door."

He gave me a skeptical glance.

"Tell me again where you were the night Lauren Alexander was killed."

He hesitated a moment, and his face tightened. "Like I told you, I met Tim at Turtles for happy hour."

"And after that?"

His face tightened with torment. "He just called me to bail him out."

"I've got news for you. When he gets arraigned, bail is going to be high on a double homicide. Are you willing to risk everything for your friend?"

He shifted uncomfortably.

"What happened after happy hour at Turtles?"

"After that, we went our separate ways. I got a call from a little hottie. I had to go take care of business. You gotta do what you gotta do, right?"

"You didn't go to Mutiny or Red November?"

He shook his head.

"Why did you lie for Timothy?"

Gareth shrugged. "I don't know. He asked me to."

"Why do you think he did that?"

"He said the cops were hassling him. He needed an alibi."

"Why would he need an alibi if he didn't do anything?" I asked.

"Because you two were up his ass."

"Innocent people don't usually arrange alibis."

"He swore to me he didn't have anything to do with it. He just got nervous when you guys started poking around. He said you guys were looking for a scapegoat. He's a little paranoid by nature. It's just the way he is."

I regarded the whole story with skepticism. "Did he mention anything to you about Lauren?"

"Yeah, he talked about her," he said, trying not to make a big deal out of it.

"A lot?"

"Okay, yeah. A lot. All the time. He wouldn't shut up about her for a while."

He stopped talking, and I gave him a look that urged him on.

"The guy was crushing hard. Then she turned him down. She used the married excuse. He was really bent about the whole thing. Then when she started banging Dylan, it was like pouring salt on the wound."

I looked at JD. A smug grin curled his face. He took great pleasure in the fact that his theory was panning out.

"Did he discuss ways to get Dylan out of the picture?" I asked.

"He talked a lot about trying to impress Lauren. I think he was scheming about how to make Dylan look like an asshole. Which wouldn't have been hard. I only met the guy once, but that was enough." Gareth paused. "Timothy didn't kill them. There's no way. He would never do something like that. I think he was trying to get Lauren to see what kind of jerk Dylan was."

"It didn't seem to bother him too much that she was married."

Gareth scoffed. "Fair game. She's the one who made the vows. If she wants to screw around, that's her choice."

"What happened to honoring the bro code?" JD said.

Gareth's face crinkled. "Sorry, old-timer. Things have changed. If some old man isn't sticking it to his wife right and she goes looking for it elsewhere, then it's open season."

"Apparently, Timothy shares your views," I said.

"If people can't keep their commitments, that's on them."

"I bet you wouldn't like it too much if somebody was sticking it to your wife," JD said.

"I'm not married. Why are you harassing me, anyway? This ain't got nothing to do with me."

I asked, "Is there anything else you're not telling us?"

26

"I'm telling you everything," Gareth said. "I swear. I just ratted out my best friend. Are you happy?"

"I'd be happy if two people weren't dead," I said.

Gareth frowned. "You think Tim really did it?"

"It's not looking good for him. I mean, do you keep remote detonators and det cord around your house?"

He shook his head.

We left the Nautilus and headed back to Diver Down. The traffic crawled. The whole island was like this now. Music blasted from car stereos, and pedestrians crammed the sidewalks. Red drink cups dangled from hands. It was faster to walk across the island than it was to drive at this time of year.

Parking was tight at the marina. Diver Down was flooded with revelers. It was everything Teagan and Alejandro could do to keep up. There wasn't any room at the bar, and the wait for a table was considerable. On the plus side, it meant revenue, and Teagan's tip jar overflowed.

My phone buzzed with a call from Isabella. It was too noisy, so I stepped outside and answered.

"You must miss me," I said.

"You have your qualities. I'll give you that. I've got something you might be interested in."

"I'm listening."

"I've been following your case on the news."

"Which one?" I chuckled.

"The Owen Patterson case. That guy was some piece of work. A lot of people lost their ass."

"It appears that way."

"Something didn't sit right with me about this since the beginning. I couldn't quite put my finger on it."

"I know what you mean."

"His Ponzi scheme was about to collapse. He transferred the money out of the exchange just in time," Isabella said. "If you hadn't seen his dead body with your own eyes, I might think he faked his death and ran off with the money."

"Owen is dead, alright. I watched divers fish him out of the water. Brenda took a close look at him."

"Well, lucky for you, I'm suspicious by nature. I've been monitoring incoming phone calls to Skyler's mother's house."

I was impressed. "You're industrious."

"She got a call. I'm pretty sure it was Skyler."

My jaw dropped. "Please tell me you have it recorded."

"I do. I'll send you the audio clip. Seems like she faked her kidnapping and bilked her boyfriend out of a metric shit ton of money."

"I gotta hand it to her—it was a pretty damn good plan," I said.

"Well, she didn't count on me. Always happy to spoil plans."

I grinned. "Thanks. You're the best."

"I know."

"Were you able to pinpoint the location of the inbound call?"

"The call wasn't encrypted, but it was bounced around the Internet through multiple proxy servers. I'm still working on it, but I'm not holding out much hope."

"Keep me posted."

"I will. This is personal. It just pisses me off. A lot of people are going to get hurt financially on this one. I'm sick of people getting fleeced by these investment scams. People work their whole lives, and their retirement evaporates in an instant."

Isabella was the wrong person to piss off. She had resources and an iron will. Not to mention, she could be cold and calculating.

A moment after I ended the call, the audio file buzzed my phone. JD and I listened to the conversation.

Wild Deceit 143

Mrs. Graham answered. "Hello?"

"Mom. It's me." I assumed it was Skyler. The voice was young and soft.

Mrs. Graham breathed a relieved sigh. "Thank God you're okay. I've been worried sick."

"I told you everything was going to be fine."

"I know, but still..."

"It's all over now. I'll send money when I can."

"When do I get to see you? I mean, am I ever going to see my daughter again?"

"Mom!"

"Sorry, but what good is all that money if you have to spend the rest of your life on the run?"

"I'm not on the run. Nobody is looking for me. They're not going to be looking for me. That's why you need to keep your mouth shut. You can't tell anyone. Not even Lori."

"You know me. I'm not going to tell anyone."

"I know you. I know how you and Lori talk after you've had a few glasses of wine."

Her mother paused. "I rarely see Lori anymore. We mostly just talk on the phone here and there."

"Not a word."

"Can I call you again on this number?"

"No. I'll call you."

"When?" her mother asked.

"When it's safe."

"Where are you?"

"It's better if you don't know."

Mrs. Graham sighed. "Owen killed himself, you know."

In a sympathetic voice, Skyler said, "I know."

There was a somber pause.

"I worry about you."

"Don't."

"I wish you hadn't done this."

"Don't start, Mom. Look, I didn't know he'd do that. It's not my fault."

"It kinda is."

"If you're gonna try to make me feel like shit, I'll hang up and won't call again."

"I just hope it was all worth it," she said in an ominous tone.

"I gotta go," Skyler said in a frustrated breath.

"Just give me a hint at where you are. Help me sleep at night. My mind is racing."

Skyler grew suspicious. "Have the police talked to you?"

"No."

"Why are you so interested in my whereabouts? Are they monitoring your calls?"

"No. I'm your mother. I'm concerned. That's all."

"How can you be sure they're not listening?"

"You said it yourself—no one is looking for you."

"Well, I'm not going to be here for long."

"You're right," Mrs. Graham huffed. "I don't want to know."

There was an awkward pause.

"Senior trip."

"What?"

"Senior trip with Kathy."

"Are you safe there?"

"Yes. Very."

"The authorities can't get you there?"

"No one's looking, remember? As long as they think I'm dead, it will stay that way. It's all taken care of."

"If you say so."

"Mom, be happy for me. Everything's going to be just fine."

"I hope so."

"It will. I'll talk to you soon."

"I love you."

"I love you too, mom."

That was the end of the call.

"I think we need to have a talk with Skyler's mother," JD said. "Figure out where Skyler went on her senior trip."

"She'll deny she talked to her daughter."

"Where do you think she's at?"

"If she was smart, she'd be in a non-extradition country."

"She seems pretty smart," JD said. "She had to have half a brain to pull this scam off."

"That call to her mother wasn't smart."

"Think we can get an international warrant?"

"Everybody thinks she's dead, and we have no proof she committed a crime. That phone call is inadmissible. We have no probable cause to believe that she is alive and has absconded with the money."

"Even more reason why we need to get her mom to crack." A mischievous smirk curled Jack's lips. "Maybe we should buy a bottle of wine and recruit Lori."

It wasn't a bad idea. But I had a simpler one.

27

My thumb almost went numb, scrolling through Skyler's *Instabook* page. I wasn't sure what I'd find, if anything at all. Don't get me wrong. Her timeline was a visual delight. Plenty of alluring photos, wearing skimpy attire in exotic locations. It was easy to see why Owen was so captivated by her. She was the kind of woman that took your breath away and deprived your brain of oxygen.

I kept scrolling through the years until I came upon photos where Skyler had tagged her friend Kathy. I knew I was getting close. I found the images of the two on white sand beaches. The tagged location was Arcadia Cay—an island in the Caribbean archipelago a little over an hour away by plane. After scrolling through a few more photos, it was clear this was their senior trip. I showed the images to JD and beamed an accomplished smile.

"Looks like we're going to Arcadia Cay."

"Sounded like she's not going to be there for long," I said.

"We might want to make this a priority."

"If we can positively identify her, maybe we can get a warrant."

"Who needs a warrant?" JD winked. "Extradition could take months or years. Call Isabella back. See if she's got any assets in the area. I'm sure that after coming into that kind of money, Skyler is going to be staying at the most expensive place on the island and dropping lots of cash."

"Unless she's smart and is lying low. If it were me, I'd keep a super low profile."

"She's already made one mistake. Let's hope she keeps on making them."

I called Isabella back and asked her to put feelers out. A woman like Skyler Graham would stick out like a sore thumb unless she tried hard to conceal herself.

Afterward, I talked to the sheriff to keep him in the loop.

"You two will do whatever you want, no matter what I say. If you go there, what are you going to do? Kidnap her and bring her back? That would be ironic."

"No. A fact-finding mission. We collect proof that she's still alive and find a way to connect her to the funds. Then we go the legit route and get an international warrant and let the marshals handle it."

Daniels scoffed. "When have you guys ever gone the legit route?"

"We go by the book all the time," I said, feigning offense.

"By the book, eh?"

"Can't argue with results," I said.

"If you go there, stay out of trouble. I won't be able to save your ass."

"Understood."

"By the way, I've got bad news. Ballistics from Desiree's gun didn't match the shooting at the Pussycat Palace."

"That's disappointing."

"You got any other leads?"

"We're working on it."

"Work harder."

"You got it, boss."

We stepped back inside Diver Down and placed a to-go order at the bar, then took our food back to the *Avventura*. We chowed down, soaking up the sun while scheming to apprehend Skyler Graham.

I got another call.

"I'm mad at you," Honey said in a pouty voice.

"What did I do?"

"You know what you did. You came by my house asking questions. Boston flipped out about Shane."

"Husbands usually do that when they learn their wife is having an affair," I said dryly.

"He would never have suspected if it weren't for you two. He kicked me out of the house."

"I'm sorry to hear that."

"I'm crashing on Lana's couch, just FYI."

"That's nice of her."

"Have you figured out who killed Shane yet?"

"No."

"What are you guys doing besides ruining my life?"

"I wish I could snap my fingers and solve cases, but I can't."

She sighed. "What are you doing right now?"

"Eating lunch."

"Meet me at the club."

"Why?"

"Do you need a reason to come see hot naked girls?"

"Not really," I said.

"Then come up to the club. I need to talk to you about something."

"We're talking right now."

"I don't want to talk about it over the phone, silly."

"Is this case related?"

"Yes. You think this is a social call?"

"You tell me."

"Don't worry. You're not my type. There's something we need to discuss."

"Alright," I sighed. "I'll stop by."

"I'm about to leave Lana's apartment now. I should be at the club in a half-hour."

"I'll see you then."

I ended the call and caught JD up to speed. A slight grin curled his face. He didn't mind going to the Palace. He didn't mind at all.

28

Sultry music thumped as we stepped into the strip club. I nodded at Bert when he saw us. He forced a smile. Bert couldn't quite figure us out. We never leaned on him or asked for anything. I'm sure that was a rarity.

I looked around the club but didn't see Honey. There were plenty of other sights to keep my eyes occupied. Voluptuous vixens tantalized enthralled customers with dances. Svelte bodies slithered. Fleshy mounds bobbled and bounced. Juicy booties found receptive laps.

The song ended, and the dancer on stage grabbed her bra and stray dollar bills that littered the mirrored floor before strutting away.

Oakley boomed into the microphone. "Give it up for Sasha!" He spun up the next tune. "Please welcome to the stage, Honey!"

The gorgeous vixen pranced on stage, her impossibly tall heels stabbing the mirrored floor. She writhed and wiggled in mesmerizing ways. She slung a toned thigh around a chrome pole and twisted. Her golden locks flowed. She performed acrobatic feats, all in rhythm to the beat. The girl knew how to work a pole, that was for sure.

"I think I'm beginning to like this job," JD said.

"Go tip her," I said.

"Don't mind if I do."

He started toward the stage with extra pep in his step. JD pulled out his money clip, peeled off a bill, and stuffed it into her G string as she knelt down beside him. They exchanged a few words, and she blew him a kiss, as she did with all her clients.

We found a table near the wall in a dim corner and enjoyed the rest of the show. Girls nearby peeled off frilly garments and danced for wide-eyed gentlemen. Buoyant assets pushed into eager faces.

The song ended, and Honey left the stage. She meandered through the club, making her way to us. She took a seat in an empty chair at our table.

"Thanks for coming," she said.

"What is it you want to talk about?"

"You're all business, aren't you?" she said with a sultry smirk. "You guys ever relax and have fun?"

"Trust me," JD said. "We always have fun."

"I bet. Like when you break up marriages? Was that fun?"

I rolled my eyes. "I don't think you can blame that solely on us."

Her eyes narrowed at me, and she exhaled through her nose. "I suppose."

"So, what do you want?"

"It's not what I want. It's what *you* want."

"What do I want?"

Her hungry gaze looked me up and down. "I bet you want a lot of things."

If I didn't know better, I might think she was flirting.

"You want information," she said.

"I'm not gonna argue with that. I want the truth."

"I think we all want the same thing. Justice for Shane."

"Agreed."

"You have to promise me something." She stared deep into my eyes.

"I don't make blind promises."

"You can't use what I'm about to tell you against Lana. She's a dear friend. She's really helping me out right now. But somebody needs to know what's going on."

"What's going on?"

"Not until you promise."

I chose my words. "Short of murder, I won't use what you tell me against Lana."

That was almost good enough for her. "Pinky swear?" She held out her dainty pinky with a French manicure. She had nice fingers.

"Pinky swear," I said, clasping her finger with mine.

She didn't break eye contact. "That's a binding agreement."

I gave her a look that said, *let's get down to business*.

She glanced around the club, then leaned in. "Lana confided in me."

"What did she say?"

Honey looked around again and flagged down a waitress.

She stopped by the table. "What can I get for you?"

"I'll take a cosmopolitan. Put it on their tab," she said, pointing to us.

The waitress asked us if we wanted anything.

"Live a little," Honey said with a naughty grin.

"Whiskey. Rocks," I said.

She looked at JD, and nobody had to twist his arm. "The same."

The waitress darted away.

I looked at Honey. "You were saying?"

"Lana and Shane got into some bad shit. I swear, I didn't know about this until today."

"What kind of bad shit?"

She hesitated. "Shane ripped off a drug dealer. Lana helped him."

"What are we talking about?" I asked. "A couple grams? A couple ounces? A couple kilos?"

"Kilos. Really good shit. I mean, not that I do a lot of coke. I mean, not often."

Something told me she was no stranger to the powdery stuff.

"Who did they steal it from?"

"I don't know. But Lana's freaking out. She thinks that's who killed Shane. She thinks she's next."

"How did this all go down?"

"Shane was buying from a guy who was getting it from a bigger dealer. Shane went with him to the stash house one time. Then he got the brilliant idea to try to cut out the middleman. When Shane went to the stash house directly, they told him to fuck off. They didn't know him. It was an invitation-only kind of deal. So Shane got the brilliant idea to case the joint and knock off the place. I guess he stole from the wrong person."

"I guess so."

Her eyes misted. She wiped the corners with the back of her hand. "I told myself I was done crying."

Despite Honey's struggle with monogamy, it was clear she had feelings for Shane. Perhaps more so than for her husband. I noticed she wasn't wearing a ring, but I wouldn't expect her to in the club. That would spoil the fantasy.

"Where's Lana now?"

"The apartment. That's why I couldn't say anything over the phone. I didn't want her to hear. She's not coming in today. She's turning into a recluse. She's afraid to leave the apartment."

The waitress returned with the drinks. JD gave her a wad of cash and a nice tip.

"Is there anything you can do?" Honey asked.

"We can talk to Lana," I said. "Try to figure out who Shane stole from."

Honey's face tightened. "You can't tell her I said anything. If you talk to her, she'll know I blabbed. Just like my husband figured something out when you talked to him."

"Did you ever stop to think that if you hadn't been fooling around, you wouldn't have any secrets to hide?"

She glared at me. "I'm sorry. He just wasn't stimulating me in that way anymore."

I raised my hands in surrender. "I'm not a marriage counselor."

"Clearly." She folded her arms and gave me a sassy look.

JD lifted his glass. "To getting to the bottom of things."

Honey joined him in a toast.

We were definitely going to get to the bottom of something if we stayed in this place too long.

The DJ spun up a new song.

"Since I'm out on my own because of you two, how about you pony up and help out with the rent?"

She stood up, unclasped her bra, and the taut fabric went slack. Her all-natural moneymakers bounced free, and she jiggled them with delight. "Which one of you wants a dance first?"

29

The sun squinted my eyes as we stepped outside the dim club. After contributing to Honey's rent, I told her to keep in touch and let me know if she learned any additional details. She told us where Lana lived and said we could probably catch her at the apartment. Despite her paranoia, she had an appointment for a cut and color later in the afternoon that she wasn't going to miss. I figured we'd do a knock and talk and see if we could get any more out of her without giving away Honey's secret.

Denise buzzed my phone. "I've got more bad news."

I groaned. "What is it?"

"Timothy killed himself."

"What!?"

"They found him dead in his cell. He used a bedsheet to hang himself. I guess he couldn't take the idea of life behind bars."

"Are you sure somebody didn't get to him?"

"No. But you want to hear the kicker? He might have walked on the charges."

"Why do you say that?"

"His prints weren't on those detonators."

"Doesn't mean anything. He wore gloves when handling them. That would be the smart thing to do."

"I don't know. Maybe you're right."

"That guy was not cut out for prison. He knew he was guilty, and he took the early release option."

"He didn't make it 24 hours."

I frowned and shook my head as I climbed into the passenger seat of the van. JD fired up the engine, and the exhaust growled.

"Thanks for the heads up," I said.

"Is that it? Is this case closed?"

"I think it's as resolved as it's gonna get."

"Daniels says you guys might be going to Arcadia Cay."

I laughed. "We might be."

"I want to go."

"This really isn't a vacation. But maybe we can all plan a trip in the future."

"That would be fun. I'm bored. I'm tired of sitting in this office. I could go with you guys and lounge around on the beach while you work. I promise I'll stay out of trouble."

The thought of Denise on a beach in a bikini created a nice visual in my mind. "Can you get the time off?"

"I can ask," she said with a hopeful voice. "I'll let you know what the boss man says."

I chuckled, and she ended the call.

We got caught in the massive inflow of traffic coming into town. It was a sea of red taillights. Cars filled to the brim with eager college students who had already started indulging in the festivities. I'm sure more than half the drivers on the road were inebriated. I'm surprised the county hadn't set up a checkpoint.

We crawled along, listening to music, taking in the circus around us. It took an hour to get to the *Babylon*. It was a luxury mid-rise complex with a visitor lot and gated under building parking—10 stories of overpriced cracker boxes.

Red and white lights from an ambulance flickered, and the warble of sirens drew near. Two patrol units screeched into the visitors' lot as we arrived.

I had a sinking feeling in the pit of my stomach.

JD found a place to park, and we hopped out of the van and hustled toward the security gate for the covered parking. A resident at the pedestrian gate let us in and ushered responders to the scene of the crime.

I grimaced when I saw the victim.

Lana had been gunned down in the parking lot as she walked to her car. She was dressed in shorts and a tank top. Her handbag was on the concrete next to her body. She was sprawled out, her limbs in unnatural positions. Her torso was riddled with multiple gunshot wounds. Crimson soaked her white shirt and pooled around her body. Tire tracks indicated she'd been run over after the fact. The bloodstained tread pattern faded toward the exit.

EMTs and paramedics rushed to Lana, donning nitrile gloves. JD and I gave them room to work as they checked her vitals and evaluated the situation.

Lana wasn't breathing, and she wasn't gonna start anytime soon.

I looked around for surveillance cameras and saw one at the far end of the parking garage. I asked the resident who let us into the garage if she had seen the incident.

"I didn't see anything until I came out to get into my car." Her voice quivered, and her face was twisted with torment. "That's when I saw her."

Her eyes welled, and she broke down in sobs.

"Did you know Lana?"

She shook her head. "I'd seen her in passing. That's all. It's a big building."

By this time, a few other residents had arrived, along with the property manager and the maintenance guy. They looked on in horror at the grizzly scene.

I surveyed the area for shell casings or any other evidence but didn't see any. JD and I looked around under nearby cars. Brass can bounce and roll quite far sometimes.

I found the property manager and asked, "Is that security camera functional?"

She nodded. "I can get you the footage if you like."

30

The property manager played back the surveillance footage from the parking garage. We huddled around her desk and watched her computer monitor.

Lana stepped into the garage from the elevator area and walked across the lane toward her car.

A man that had been lurking behind the wall by the elevator entrance stepped into frame. He took aim and squeezed off several rounds.

Geysers of blood erupted as bullets peppered Lana's back. She twitched and convulsed with each hit.

Brass casings pinged as they bounced against the concrete, echoing off the walls.

The property manager turned away and couldn't keep watching.

A black Camaro, parked a few cars down, screeched out of a space and into the lane.

The shooter knelt down, picked up his hot brass with gloved hands, then climbed into the passenger seat of the Camaro. He wore a black hat and sunglasses. A bandana covered his face. From the video, he looked 5'8"- 5'10", medium build.

The driver mashed the gas, and tires squealed. The vehicle ran over Lana's body, bouncing over her like a speed bump, leaving a trail of bloody tracks.

The Camaro rounded the corner, and the automatic gate opened when they hit the pressure pad. The vehicle sped away.

The license plate had been removed.

It was a shocking act of violence. A ruthless display of power. If these were the drug dealers that Lana and Shane had stolen from, they were sending a message. Whether they got the drugs back was irrelevant. *Steal from us, and you die* is what the message said.

The property manager exported the clip and sent me a download link. I forwarded it to the department and downloaded the clip to my phone. I got her contact info, gave her my card, and told her we'd be in touch.

We left the office and made our way back down to the garage. By that time, Brenda and her crew had arrived, and the forensic team combed the garage for evidence.

I took another look around the parking lot and searched for any stray shell casings in the area where the shooter was.

I didn't see anything.

Paris Delaney and her crew had weaseled their way into the secured parking garage and were soaking up footage of the horrid scene.

I called Honey, but she didn't answer.

I sent her a text message and informed her of the incident and told her she might not want to come back to the apartment. I didn't know if she was mixed up in this or not. I figured the thugs would take out anyone they suspected of being a party to the theft. For her sake, I hoped she wasn't involved.

Dietrich snapped photos, and camera flashes bounced around the garage.

Everything was documented and chronicled.

When Brenda had completed her assessment, her team bagged the body and loaded it onto a gurney. Lana's remains were wheeled out of the garage and stuffed into the back of the medical examiner's van.

Paris accosted us on the way out of the garage. The camera closed in, and the fluffy boom microphone hovered overhead. A light atop the camera shined in my eyes.

"Deputy Wild, what can you tell us about this tragic shooting?"

"I can't discuss anything at this time."

"Is this gang-related?"

I shrugged.

"Were there drugs involved?"

We had a leak in the department, and I wasn't sure how much information Paris already had. But with this type of shooting, it was a safe bet that criminal cartels, gangs, and drugs were involved.

We headed back to the station and filled out after-action reports. By the time we wrapped up, we needed to get ready for the show at *Taffy Beach*. We hustled across the island to the warehouse and met Floyd and Pinky, the two roadies that I had hired.

They loaded all the gear into the van, and we headed to the beach.

The festivities had been going on all day and would continue well into the night. It would be like this every day for the next three weeks. There were bands, DJs, bikini contests, and wet T-shirt contests, among other things. Dozens and dozens of acts were booked to play the festival over the next few weeks, and Wild Fury was scheduled to headline a few nights. The frenetic pace was so intense there was no time for a sound check. When it was time to change the stage over, the crew would load the gear on, make sure everything was mic'd up, and test the levels. The guy running sound had worked with us a number of times before. He was the regular guy at Sonic Temple. He knew the band and our set well, so I was relatively confident things would go off without a hitch.

As a sponsor of the festival, the Wild Fury Whiskey logo was everywhere—on banners across the stage and alongside the towering speakers.

Wild Fury didn't go on until 10 PM. They were scheduled to play until 11, when things would shut down due to the noise ordinance. Floyd and Pinky stayed with the gear while we met the guys for dinner at *The Lobster House*. Jack always liked to give them a good meal before going on stage.

We filled our bellies, then pre-gamed at Red November, then made our way to Taffy Beach.

It was 9:30 PM when we arrived, and the place was packed. The beach was a sea of bodies. Sunburned faces and shoulders. Sandy bottoms and sloppy drunks. This crowd had been drinking all day long. I was surprised this many were still standing.

There was a first-aid tent at the far end of the beach. They treated revelers for dehydration, heat stress, and alcohol-induced issues. Of course, there was the occasional drug overdose. There was a lot of ecstasy going around this Spring Break. Some of it good, some of it not so good, and some of it wasn't ecstasy at all—a mixture of methamphetamine and other drugs. Sometimes kids would take a pill on a full stomach, and it wouldn't hit them as fast as they'd like, so they'd take another. Then when it kicked in, it was too much.

There was the occasional brawl that had to be dealt with and the unfortunate incidents of sexual assault and groping. That came with every Spring Break. But by and large, I hadn't heard of anything out of the ordinary this year. Though, what was ordinary for Coconut Key could often be outrageous.

The Royal Peasants opened for us, and they came off the stage at 9:45 PM. It was just barely enough time to get the stage turned around and everything set up.

It was 10:20 PM by the time I took the stage to introduce the band. Spotlights illuminated me as I grabbed the microphone. I scanned the endless sea of bodies. "Are we having fun, or are we having fun?"

The drunken crowd roared.

"Well, you ain't seen nothing yet. Please welcome to the stage, the mighty, Wild Fury!"

The crowd went wild. Women screamed, and men whistled.

Dizzy struck a power cord on the guitar, buzzing through massive speakers.

The guys rushed onto the stage. Crash thundered a baseline. Styxx climbed behind his candy-apple red drum set and started beating the crap out of it.

I exited stage-left, and Jack howled into the microphone. "Are you ready to rock 'n' roll!?"

The question was met with a deafening roar from the audience.

"I can't hear you! Are you ready to rock and roll!?"

The drunkards screamed even louder.

"That's more like it!"

Styxx clicked off the beat, and the band broke into *Fast Love*. A freight train of sound pummeled the crowd from the tower of speakers on either side of the stage. Colored lights from the grid above swirled in a precise movement in sync with the beat.

Suddenly, a deafening bang thundered the stage, like a cannon!

It wasn't a good bang, either.

The lights went out, and the sound died.

31

Something had blown, and the power went down. With the death threats the band had gotten, I was concerned for a moment until I figured out what was going on.

I grabbed a bullhorn and shouted at the unsettled audience. I asked them to remain calm and told them it would only be a moment while we tried to resolve the technical difficulties. I hoped we could get things up and rolling. Otherwise, we'd have quite a few disappointed fans.

It took 30 minutes to get the power back up. By that time, the band would have 10 minutes to play until the noise ordinance kicked in.

Not to be deterred, Wild Fury resumed their set and played until 11:30 PM. We had a little pull with the county but eventually had to shut it down.

JD finished the set by thanking the audience and telling them Wild Fury would be back in a couple of days to play another show.

Pinky and Floyd broke down the gear on stage, loaded it into the van, and took it back to the warehouse.

We lingered around backstage until they returned. By that time, the guys had rounded up a few eager participants for an after-party, and we all made our way back to the *Avventura*.

Pinky and Floyd joined—perks of the business.

A good time was had by all.

Daniels called in the morning with good news for once. "As we figured, the ballistics in the Lana Brooks shooting matched the Shane Jeffries case. Gives a little credibility to that stripper's story about them knocking off a drug dealer."

"Now we just need to figure out who the drug dealer is," I said.

"We might have a lead. A guy that lives in Lana's apartment complex called the department. He noticed a shell casing stuck in his tire tread. The forensic team analyzed the casing, pulled a partial print, and we ran it through the system. Got a hit on a guy named Lennox Bradley. He's got priors for possession, assault, and resisting arrest. Echols issued a warrant. I want you to put together a tac team and pick him up."

"With pleasure," I said with a grin.

I ended the call, pulled myself out of bed, and went through my morning routine. After I got dressed, I hustled down the steps to the main deck and banged on the hatch to JD's stateroom. I shouted, "Get up. We've got people to arrest."

I slipped into the galley and started grilling breakfast. The boat looked like a bomb had gone off, as usual. The deal was the guys could party on the boat, but they had to clean up. They were pretty good about it for the most part, but I often beat them to it.

JD stumbled out of his stateroom a few minutes later, and we chowed down. Afterward, we headed to the station, suited up in tactical gear, and had a pre-mission briefing with Mendoza, Robinson, Erickson, and Faulkner.

We drove the van, and they followed in patrol cars to 837 Redfin Lane. It was a small one-story bungalow with white siding and forest-green shutters. There were a few plants in the yard and a couple short, thick palms.

We parked a few houses down and surveyed the suspect's property. A black Camaro was parked at the curb. It sure looked like the vehicle in the surveillance footage from Lana's parking garage.

We hopped out of the van and crept toward the house.

Erickson and Faulkner raced up the driveway to cover the rear. Robinson and Mendoza joined us to breach the front. We all had wireless earbuds, and Faulkner signaled when his team was in position.

Mendoza and Robinson readied the battering ram.

JD and I took a position on either side of the front door.

Jack pounded his fist and shouted, "Coconut County. We have a warrant!"

With that, Mendoza and Robinson heaved the battering ram against the door. Wood splintered, and the doorjamb fractured. Glass shattered, and diamond-like shards rained down.

The door swung wide.

JD tossed a flash-bang grenade inside.

It bounced across the tile and popped with a deafening bang. The living room filled with smoke and haze.

I angled my pistol into the foyer and advanced.

Gunfire erupted, and muzzle flash flickered through the haze.

Bullets snapped past me down the foyer, whizzing inches from my flesh.

I returned fire, but the thud of an impact sounded behind me.

That horrible sensation twisted in my gut.

Someone had been hit.

32

Mendoza took a hit to the chest. It knocked him on his ass and pushed the air out of his lungs.

Adrenaline and rage pumped through me. I returned fire while JD grabbed Mendoza and pulled him onto the porch, out of harm's way.

The acrid smoke from the flash-bang grenade filled my nostrils, mixed with the scent of gunpowder as my pistol hammered my palm.

I hit one of the bastards in the living room. He tumbled back and fell into the flatscreen.

Blood spewed from his chest.

He smacked the ground, and his weapon clattered away.

The 65" flatscreen crashed down on top of him, covering his face and torso with a crunch.

His companion, Lennox, had fled through the back door.

Gunshots erupted as he engaged Erickson and Faulkner.

A hail of bullets crisscrossed the backyard.

The thug bolted around the corner of the house, haphazardly firing at the deputies the entire time.

Despite the close quarters, none of the bullets hit their targets.

It wasn't unusual. 90% of shots taken within 10 feet miss their target. Adrenaline degrades fine motor skills.

I backtracked out of the house and caught sight of the perp darting out of the alley between houses. Lennox's wide eyes glanced at me as he bolted to the street and ran away.

"Is he going to be okay?" I asked JD in a hurried breath.

"I don't know," he replied, applying pressure to Mendoza's wound.

The bullet had pierced the vest and pulverized flesh.

Mendoza's skin was slick with sweat, and his wide eyes filled with fear. He was going into shock.

"Hang in there," JD urged. "Help is on the way."

Anger swelled, and I took off after the thug.

Lennox sprinted down the street, his sneakers slapping against the concrete. He raced past parked cars, under rows of towering palm trees.

Lennox angled his pistol over his shoulder and fired a few careless shots at me.

Bullets snapped through the air, and I ducked cover behind a parked Honda.

The perp kept running down the block and took a right at the stop sign on Palmdale. It was a narrow throughway. Green trash bins lined the road. Tall palms and live oaks shaded the residential street.

I followed and rounded the corner.

Lennox sprinted toward the next intersection.

A kid on an electric scooter zipped around the corner, heading toward us.

The thug put an elbow into the kid's face and knocked him off the scooter.

Blood spewed from the kid's nose, and his back smacked the concrete. With the wind knocked out of him, he instantly burst into tears while simultaneously gasping for breath.

I wanted to beat Lennox senseless.

The unmanned scooter careened down the road and finally crashed halfway between me and the thug.

I don't think Lennox expected it to roll that far away. He took a few steps toward it, then thought better of it as I advanced.

Then he did exactly as I feared.

He ran to the kid, yanked him to his feet, and put his pistol to the kid's head.

Blood flowed from the boy's nose as he sobbed. Tears mixed with bloody snot. He was maybe 14 or 15.

"Back off, or he dies!"

33

I froze in my tracks. No way was I going to risk anything happening to the boy.

"Put your weapon down!" Lennox shouted.

I carefully squatted down and set my pistol on the ground, then stood up with my hands in the air.

Lennox dragged the kid to the intersection just as a minivan arrived at the stop sign. He swung the barrel of his pistol toward the driver and pulled the kid in front of the grill. "Get out of the car! Now!"

Terrified, the woman behind the wheel complied. She flung open the door and stepped out of the vehicle. But she forgot to put it in park.

The minivan idled forward.

Lennox darted out of the way, releasing the kid.

The boy took off running toward me, and Lennox hopped behind the wheel of the minivan, stomped the gas, and took off around the corner.

Tires squealed.

Lennox pulled the driver's door shut as the minivan barreled down the street.

I grabbed my gun and rushed to the kid. "Are you okay?"

He nodded.

I called for backup and gave a description of the minivan and the plate number.

I checked on the frazzled woman. She was mid-40s with curly auburn hair and a round face. She trembled from the incident but was unharmed.

By this time, Erickson and Faulkner had caught up with me. They took over with the woman, and I asked the kid where he lived.

He said, "Just down the street."

"I'll walk you home."

I righted his scooter. The tank was scuffed, and the ends of the handlebars were raw. I rolled it back to the kid's house and parked it at the curb.

The kid went inside and got his mother.

She freaked out.

I filled her in on the situation.

The boy had scuffs and scrapes, but I didn't think his nose was broken. "I can call an ambulance, if you like? Or you can take him to a minor emergency center."

"I think he's okay." She was an attractive brunette, nearing 40, with short hair. "Thank you for bringing him back to me."

"It was a lucky break."

"I'll take luck any day."

I gave her my card and hustled back to the Lennox's house. By that time, an ambulance had taken Mendoza to the hospital, as well as the scumbag that I shot in the living room, Omar Paxton.

More patrol cars were on the scene with flashing lights, and a crowd of curious neighbors gawked.

Deputies searched the house and found a couple Mac-10s, some weed, and a little cocaine. Forensic investigators scoured the Camaro, looking for blood and other trace evidence.

Paris Delaney and crew were on the scene, soaking up the drama and intrigue.

I asked JD, "What's the word on Mendoza?"

He shrugged, and a grim look tightened his face.

34

The ER was packed, mostly from alcohol-related incidents, a few overdoses, and participants of a few brawls. The pale fluorescents bathed the waiting area in a sickly glow.

There were broken bones, runny noses, and a few elderly on supplemental oxygen. It was always a depressing place. A 24-hour news channel droned on the flatscreen mounted to the wall near the ceiling. Kids at a table played with toys.

We waited with Erickson, Faulkner, and Robinson while Mendoza underwent emergency surgery.

Omar Paxton was in the OR as well, still clinging to life. Lennox Bradley was on the run. Daniels had put out a BOLO on the vehicle and the perp. The sheriff joined us in the ER to await the outcome of Mendoza's surgery.

Coconut General was a Level I trauma center, and Mendoza was in the best of hands with Dr. Parker. Still, penetrating thoracic wounds are nasty business. Blood loss, secondary to the initial trauma, is the leading cause of mortality.

It didn't make sense to me. The thugs had used small caliber, 9mm rounds. The newly issued vests should have been more than capable of stopping a bullet at that distance.

"I want to know what the hell happened," Daniels said with a tight jaw. "I want everybody using their old vests until we sort this out."

"We never switched over," I said.

"Well, sometimes you two are smarter than you look."

It was over an hour later when Dr. Parker emerged. He pushed through the double doors, the surgical mask still over his face. His teal scrubs were stained with blood. He held Mendoza's vest in his hand. It had been removed by emergency responders.

Parker was a hard man to read, especially with the mask covering his face.

We launched from our chairs and hustled to greet him, waiting for his report with bated breath.

"Well, he's going to make it," Dr. Parker said.

Relief washed over us.

"He's got a rib fracture and a pulmonary contusion, along with a hemothorax. I went in laparoscopically and found a splenic and renal laceration, and we had to resect part of the descending colon. At this time, I don't think his spleen will need to come out, but we'll keep an eye on it. They like to bleed."

"Thank you," I said.

"I'm going to say what I always say. If you boys would keep from getting shot, it sure would make my job a lot easier." He handed me the vest. "This didn't seem to do much."

I examined the vest, and my jaw tightened. I plunged my finger through the hole in the synthetic fabric.

"Who the hell manufactured that thing?" Daniels grumbled.

I searched for the label and grumbled when I read it. I can't say I was surprised. I showed it to the sheriff.

His jaw tightened. "Somebody's got some explaining to do."

"What about the perp, Omar Paxton?" I asked Parker.

"You'll have to talk to Dr. Khan when he gets out of surgery. If you want to stick around."

"When can we see Mendoza?"

"He's in recovery right now and still pretty groggy. He'll be admitted, and I suspect he'll be in the hospital for quite a while. A few weeks, at least. Go home. Get some rest. Come back in the morning."

I thanked him again, and we shook hands.

Paris Delaney stood outside the emergency room, commenting on camera about the incident. She noticed us when we stepped outside, and the crew rushed in for questions.

"Can you tell us the current status of Deputy Mendoza?"

I informed her that he was in critical but stable condition. "We're asking for anyone with information as to the whereabouts of Lennox Bradley to contact the Coconut County

Sheriff's Department immediately. Do not try to apprehend the suspect yourself."

"What's the status of the other suspect?"

"I don't know."

I stepped out of frame.

Paris would be the first person on my list if I needed to publicize the faulty vest.

We returned to the station, filled out after-action reports, and I surrendered my duty weapon. I was put on administrative leave pending the outcome of an investigation. It was standard operating procedure.

"I want you to get to the bottom of this vest fiasco," Daniels said. "And pronto. Heads are gonna roll."

35

Despite being put on leave, I wasn't about to let this one go. I was still riled up about the incident, as was everyone else.

JD and I drove over to ARMG Unlimited and stormed into the lobby. I flashed my badge to the receptionist, even though she knew who we were. "I need to speak with Noah Benson immediately."

She shifted uncomfortably. "I think he's in a meeting right now. Can I tell him what this is in regard to?"

"I just have a few additional questions."

She forced a smile. "Give me one moment."

She buzzed his extension. "Noah, the deputies are here to see you again." She listened intently to his reply.

I thought we were going to get the runaround again.

"Great. I'll tell them." She ended the call and said to us, "He says he'll see you now. You can find him at the end of the hall," she pointed.

I gave a nod of appreciation, and we marched to Noah's office. My knuckles tapped the door before pushing it open.

Noah stood up from behind the desk with a smile. "Gentlemen. It's a pleasure. What can I do for you?"

"You can tell me about the faulty bulletproof vests your company sold our department."

Confusion twisted his face. "What do you mean?"

"I mean, one of our deputies was almost killed today."

He lifted his brow with surprise. "That's terrible. What happened?"

"It seems your vest didn't perform as advertised."

"As unfortunate as it may be, these vests are not rated to withstand every type of round. High-caliber and armor-piercing bullets can present a challenge."

"Your vest should stop a 9mm bullet at 30 feet, shouldn't it?"

"It should." He paused and went into damage control mode. "I can see you're upset."

"Damn right, I'm upset."

"Understandably so. You have every right to be. Do you have the vest in question?"

"It's at the department for analysis."

"If you can get it to me, I'll look into the matter. Perhaps there was a defect in manufacturing. I'm sure there's a logical explanation for what happened. Again, I'm very sorry, and I hope your friend is okay."

"He's got a long recovery ahead of him."

"If you can give me the serial number, I can look up the batch and investigate."

"Something tells me you're going to get a lot of these back."

He tried to hide his displeasure at the thought of a potential recall. "I know that nothing is going to undo the trauma that your colleague has faced. But I give you my word. I will get to the bottom of this and do everything I can to make the situation right."

I called the sheriff and asked him to look up the production number of the vest. I relayed that information to Noah. He scribbled it down on a notepad and assured us he would look into things.

I contained my anger as best I could. A lot of things could have gone wrong. A design flaw. A manufacturing defect. Sometimes these things happen. I couldn't necessarily blame Noah.

"Again, please accept my apologies. Tell me about the deputy. I would like to offer my personal assistance to his family during this difficult time."

I gave him Deputy Mendoza's name and information. He seemed genuine.

"I know you gentlemen put your lives in our hands when you utilize products like this to ensure your safety. If this turns out to be a fault on our end, then we let you down. I can assure you, we will make the situation right."

"I appreciate your consideration."

"Did your department purchase the vests directly from us, or a retailer?"

"You should call the sheriff and speak with him directly."

"I will. Is there anything else I can do for you, gentlemen?"

"Not at this time." Then I added, "I'm sure you've heard about Timothy."

He frowned and shook his head. "Such a shame. I never would have thought him capable of such a thing." He sighed. "I don't know what's going on these days. It seems like one thing after another. I don't know about you, but I'm ready for a little good news."

There was a long pause.

"If you'll excuse me, gentlemen, I have a videoconference I need to jump on."

He extended his hand, and we shook before leaving.

We strolled the hallway toward the reception desk, moving past other offices. My tone had been loud and angry, and I'm sure it filtered through the walls. We drew curious stares from other executives on the way out.

"Good afternoon, gentlemen," the receptionist said to us as we left.

I had no doubt that if the vest was indeed faulty, there would be a hell of a lawsuit.

We left the building, hopped into the van, and braved the traffic on our way back to Diver Down. It wasn't quite happy hour yet, but it was close enough. I was off for the rest of the day and ready to unwind.

The place was packed. Teagan and Alejandro were in the weeds.

We squeezed to the bar counter.

Teagan knew what we were after. She poured two glasses of whiskey and slid them across the counter. A concerned look tensed her face. "I've got something for you," she said to Jack. "At least, I hope it's for you and not me."

She slid a folded piece of paper across the counter. It was a little larger than a business card, torn into a rectangle by hand. JD unfolded the paper and his face twisted with a scowl.

36

You failed to listen to my warning. Now I must kill, the note read.

It had been formed with cut-out letters, arranged carefully, then photographed and printed on an inkjet. Just like the previous note.

"Who do you think sent this?" JD asked.

"Your girlfriend," I teased.

"She's not my girlfriend." His mouth scrunched. "And she didn't send this. Somebody would have spotted her." He paused. "Any word from the lab about that other note?"

"Printed on a Capson E365 inkjet printer. Paper can be bought from any major office supply."

JD glanced around the bar, uneasy. "Whoever it is walked in here and stuffed it in Teagan's tip jar. They know where we live." He paused. "Why don't you have security cameras in this place?"

"People bitch about them. They want to come here and drink in privacy. Start putting cameras in here, and in the parking lot, and people think you're gonna bust them for DUI or that there's going to be video evidence of an affair or something they'd rather not have on camera. That's why I don't keep video cameras around here. I like this bar, and I like my customers."

JD frowned, still keeping a watchful eye.

"I think somebody's messing with your head."

"They're starting to do a good job of it."

"It could be anybody. With the number of perps we've put away, there are a lot of pissed-off people out there. There are a lot of pissed-off friends and relatives of people we've put away. Not to mention the people that want to see us dead from our former lives."

"Speak for yourself. I'm too adorable to kill."

"So you've said."

My phone buzzed my pocket. I pulled out the device and looked at the screen. It was the Match for Life Center. I had registered as a donor in case I was a match for someone who needed a bone marrow transplant. Paris Delaney's niece was in dire need of the procedure, and none of her immediate family members were a genetic match. There were all kinds of risks for the patient, and the better the match, the lower the risk that the patient would reject the new stem cells. Her niece had a rare blood disorder, aplastic anemia, and if she didn't get a bone marrow transplant, the odds of survival weren't good.

I stepped outside and took the call.

A cheery woman asked, "Is this Tyson Wild?"

"It is."

"Hi, I'm Sheryl with Match for Life. I'm calling to let you know that you've been identified as a potential match for a specific patient."

"Fantastic."

"You have a wonderful opportunity to help someone suffering from a life-threatening blood disorder. I hope you're still willing to proceed."

"I am."

"I just want you to know that you're giving someone hope. This is a potentially life-saving transplant. The patient's doctor has requested additional testing to confirm that you're an appropriate match. All we need from you is a simple blood draw. You will be asked to sign a consent form and complete a health questionnaire. You still have the option not to move forward at any time. So there's no obligation after this round of testing. Of course, we hope you will continue to move forward. You decided to join the registry because you're obviously passionate about saving lives."

"Indeed. No worries. What do I need to do?"

"I can schedule you for next week at a local testing center in Coconut Key. Do you have a time preference?"

"How's 10 AM?"

"Perfect. Let me see what's available."

We went back and forth on times and dates, finally settling on one.

"I'll send you a confirmation text with the address. If you need to cancel or reschedule, please just let us know. Again, I want to thank you for your participation."

"My pleasure."

"I also want to reiterate that just because you've made it to this phase does not necessarily mean that you will be a perfect match, but we remain hopeful."

She thanked me again, and I ended the call.

At this point, I had no way of knowing who the potential match was. The whole process was geared around patient and donor privacy. It could have been Paris's niece or somebody else entirely. It was a national registry serving the needs of patients all over the country and even across the globe.

The test was a simple blood draw for me. If I was a match, it was life for somebody else. A no-brainer and not much of a sacrifice.

I stepped back inside and filled JD in on the call.

He lifted his glass. "To saving lives."

We clinked glasses and sipped the fine whiskey, taking in the scenery. There were lots of jean shorts and bikini tops.

My phone buzzed with a call from Denise. I answered and stepped back outside so I could hear.

"Hey, a guy just called the department looking for you. Says he has information about Lauren Alexander. He wouldn't say his name or give his number. I gave him yours, and he says he will call from a pay phone shortly."

37

My phone buzzed with a call from a random number. I swiped the screen.

"Is this Deputy Wild?" a man asked.

"It is. I understand you have information to share."

"I think I know who's responsible for Lauren's death."

"I'm listening."

"I heard about the deputy that was shot. I couldn't bite my tongue any longer. Those vests are defective, and the company knew about it. Lauren brought it to Noah's attention, but he dismissed it. She threatened to go public if he didn't recall the vests."

"I assume you work for the company?"

"I do."

"What's your name?"

"I'd rather not say. Not yet, anyway."

"Do you have any proof?"

"Yes. Lauren had collected all the data. The vests worked great at first. All the initial testing was flawless. But the synthetic fibers broke down over time. By the time they were manufactured, stored, and shipped, they were worthless. Any information about the failures was suppressed by the company."

"Where's the data?"

"I have it on a USB drive. Lauren didn't trust the cloud or her personal devices. They all belong to the company. They know everything we do. Every email. Every phone call. That's why I'm calling you from a pay phone. I've got my cell turned off right now. I wouldn't be surprised if they've got it bugged. I don't even want to have private conversations with the phone in the same room. Phone mics can be activated remotely and used as listening devices."

"I'm aware. Can you get me a copy of the USB drive?"

"No. I'll just give you the drive. I'm not plugging that into my computer. I'm totally paranoid. They're watching everything."

"Let's meet in person," I said. "You can give me the USB drive."

He hesitated for a moment. "Okay. Meet me at Dunsel in 30 minutes. I want to get rid of this."

"How will I recognize you?"

"I'll recognize you."

I ended the call, went back inside, and informed JD. He was chatting up two lovely young ladies.

"Will you be here later?" he asked the blonde. "We have to run an errand."

"We might stick around," she said with a delightful smile.

JD collected their info.

We left Diver Down, and I hustled to the *Avventura* to get a backup. I was technically on leave, but I wasn't going to walk around unarmed. I rejoined JD in the parking lot. Jack climbed behind the wheel of the van and cranked up the beast. He put it into gear, backed out of the space, and rolled out of the lot.

We drove to Dunsel and found a place to park. It took almost half an hour to get there with traffic. Dunsel was off the beaten path, far from the tourist traps of Oyster Avenue. It was a neighborhood hole-in-the-wall filled with regulars. Nothing to write home about, but a great place to get a cheap drink, play pool, throw darts, and spill your sorrows on anyone who would listen.

We stepped inside the dim club. Classic rock filtered from the jukebox. To the right were pool tables and dartboards. A long bar spanned almost the length of the club. To the left was a row of booths. Restrooms and a payphone were in the back.

The bar was pretty full. I had no idea who our informant was.

JD and I grabbed a seat at two empty bar stools.

The bartender made his way to us. "What can I get you, gentlemen?"

"Whiskey. Rocks," JD said.

"Make that two," I added.

"You Deputy Wild?" the bartender asked.

I nodded with a quizzical expression. We'd been in the bar a few times before, but I didn't know his name, and I didn't think he knew mine.

The bartender dug into his pocket, pulled out a USB drive, and slid it across the counter. "I was asked to give this to you."

I examined the drive, then slipped it into my pocket.

"I was told that two gentlemen would be coming in here that fit your description. You guys are kind of hard to miss."

JD stuck out like a sore thumb with his long blond hair and loud Hawaiian shirt.

"Who gave you the drive?" I asked.

The bartender smiled. "A good bartender keeps secrets."

He poured two glasses of whiskey, slid them across the counter, and said, "This one's on the house."

We lifted our glasses in appreciation.

I surveyed the bar, looking for anyone out of place.

A guy in his late 20s at the far end fit the bill. He climbed off his bar stool and headed toward the exit. He wore a slick *Di Fiore* suit, which was a little high-end for this place. His brown hair was well-styled, and he seemed like a bit of a fashionista. I recognized him as an executive at ARMG. I didn't speak with him when I was on the premises, but I saw him in an office down the hall from Noah's after I'd burst into the CEO's office and read him the Riot Act.

Slick's nervous eyes flicked to me for an instant as he passed. He marched out of the bar and into the parking lot.

I told JD, "I think that was our informant."

"He is a little on the paranoid side."

"Can you blame him? A little healthy paranoia will keep you alive."

"You think there's anything to his story?"

"We're about to find out. I say we head back to the Avventura, pop this into the computer, and see what we're dealing with."

JD left a tip for the bartender, and we stepped outside. The night air swirled. The stars flickered above, and the moon presided.

A black Denali SUV clicked on its lights and launched from a parking space. The engine roared as the vehicle raced near us, then slowed. A black submachine gun emerged from the passenger window.

38

Muzzle flash flickered from the barrel.

Bullets spewed.

The deafening clatter of gunfire echoed across the parking lot.

I watched the whole thing unfold in slow motion. The thug with the machine gun wore dark sunglasses and had a black neoprene face mask with a white skull printed on it.

The right front quarter panel and door had silver scrapes on it.

I grabbed JD and pulled him to the ground with me, taking cover behind a car that was parked nose to the curb.

We crouched by the grill as molten copper shattered windshields, pelted body panels, and smacked into the brickwork of the building behind us.

Metal popped and pinged.

Diamond-like shards rained down.

The gunfire ended, and tires squealed as the vehicle launched away.

I drew my pistol, popped up over the hood of the car, and returned fire. My pistol hammered against my palm, and the tangy scent of gunpowder filled my nostrils. My bullets smacked the rear of the SUV, taking out a taillight and putting a few holes in body panels. I put a few through the back window, webbing it with cracks.

The vehicle blazed out of the parking lot, turning onto the road, laying down streaks of rubber.

There were no plates on the SUV.

"I'm pretty sure that's the same vehicle that ran Lauren off the road," I said while catching my breath, my heart punching my chest. Adrenaline spiked my nerves, and my skin was alive.

Nothing like a little contact with the enemy to perk you up.

"I think somebody doesn't want us to have that USB drive," JD said.

"You okay?" I asked.

Jack nodded.

I looked him over for blossoming crimson and gave myself a quick pat down, feeling for blood. Sometimes adrenaline can mask the initial pain.

I called the sheriff and informed him of the situation. He put a BOLO out on the vehicle.

A couple patrol cars arrived on the scene, lights flashing.

Fortunately, nobody had been hurt, but there was plenty of property damage.

The forensic team arrived, went over the vehicles, and recovered a few slugs. Bullets were embedded in the vehicles and the brickwork.

JD and I went to the station and filled out after-action reports. I logged the drive into evidence and had the IT guys make a copy of it for me. We pulled up the contents and started sifting through it. There were multiple reports about the degradation of the synthetic material when combined with another chemical during the manufacture of the vests. The drive contained several copies of emails Lauren had sent to Noah informing him of this, and there was even a video clip of Lauren confronting the CEO. She had worn a spycam during the meeting.

We played the clip:

"Thank you. This is interesting," Noah said, looking over the reports. "Where did you get this information?"

"I can't say," Lauren replied.

His face tightened. "You can't, or you won't?"

"What does it matter? The results indicate we have a problem."

"So, an outside lab evaluates our product, and you assume it's accurate? This could be a bogus report sponsored by a competitor. How were the tests conducted? What was their methodology?"

"It's a reputable lab."

"I will definitely do a deep dive and get to the bottom of this."

"I think this requires more than a deep dive," Lauren said in a sharp tone. "This warrants a product recall."

Noah smiled. "Let's not get ahead of ourselves. We've got dozens of other tests and data points that show these vests are working as intended. It's the most lightweight and flexible IIIA armor you can buy. They're certified, and we've demonstrated effectiveness up to .44 magnum rounds."

"All of those tests were done before the material had the opportunity to degrade," Lauren said. "Something is weakening the fibers. Likely the bonding agent between the layers. The certification board's follow-up testing may or may not catch this defect, depending on the age of the random samples they test. We can't, in good conscience, ship these vests until we know exactly what's going on."

"Could just be a bad batch. An isolated incident. This could be a manufacturing defect that in no way has anything to do with the design of the product. Or this could be a competitor trying to sabotage our brand."

"Are you suggesting that the outside lab could have been bribed to make a false report?"

Noah shrugged. "Wherever there is a human element involved, there is a possibility for corruption. That's why I will dig into this data and make an evaluation."

"If there is a bad batch, we need to track it down and recall it."

"A recall at this stage of rollout could be devastating for sales. It would irreparably damage the product's image and the company's reputation."

"And what do you think is going to happen when people start dying from a faulty product that we manufacture?"

He forced a calm response. "I believe these vests offer adequate protection when worn properly and used in the manner intended."

"Are you not listening to me?"

"I appreciate you bringing this to my attention, and I will take it under advisement. Rest assured, if there is an issue, I will track the faulty batch down and have samples tested before they are shipped."

"They may already have shipped," Lauren said.

"I'll handle this," Noah assured.

"If you're not going to do something, I will," Lauren threatened.

"What does that mean?" Noah asked, his eyes narrowing at her.

"It means what it means."

Noah's jaw tightened. "Who else have you talked to about this?"

"I'm bringing it to you first."

"And I appreciate that. I promise you, this will get sorted. What I don't need is rumors circulating about the safety and effectiveness of our products. And, may I remind you of the non-disclosure agreement you signed upon your employment."

"I'm well aware of my obligations."

Noah forced a smile. "Well, I'm glad we're on the same page. Now, if you'll excuse me, I have matters to attend to."

Lauren left Noah's office in a huff, and I paused the video.

"What a scumbag," JD grumbled. "Mendoza's sitting in a hospital bed fighting for his life because of that dirtball."

Jack's cheeks reddened, and his veins started to bulge.

"He was made aware that the product was faulty," I said. "There's data here to back it up."

"He'll pay a high-powered attorney and an expert witness to say that everything is fine and the outside testing is flawed. There's no way anybody does any time over this. They never do. These bigwigs get a slap on the wrist, a fine, and it's back to business as usual." JD's jaw clenched. "I guarantee you he had Lauren killed. Dylan was probably an innocent bystander. And he sent those ass-clowns to gun us down. I don't know about you, but I'm in the mood for a little payback."

Bringing down Noah Benson shot to the top of my priorities list. If I couldn't get him on anything else, fraud would have to do. But JD was right. This thing could get tied up in the courts for a decade and still not lead to the desired outcome.

The situation was complicated. The vests were partially funded by a grant from the Justice Department as part of their Bulletproof Vest Partnership program. Since 1999, over a million vests have been funded. That made this a federal matter. ARMG was a GSA provider, and this fell under the purview of the GSA's Office of the Inspector General.

I contacted the OIG and informed them of the situation. I wasn't big on handing over cases, but there was no telling how many other agencies and departments had been defrauded. I was certain DCIS, Homeland Security, the Defense Contracting Audit Agency, and numerous other special investigative departments would get involved.

How slow or fast they would move on this was anyone's guess.

I had no doubt Paris would catch wind of this soon. But I didn't want to spook Noah until we had built a solid case. I debated whether to make a preemptive call, asking her to sit on the story. Not that she would listen. The ambitious reporter certainly had a mind of her own.

Daniels caught up with us in the conference room. "You two are supposed to be on administrative leave. Instead, you guys get in a firefight at a bar."

"Outside a bar," I clarified. "Somebody tried to kill us. Don't worry, we're okay."

He scowled at me, not amused by my dry wit.

"You're lucky nobody died. It doesn't look good when a suspended deputy shoots somebody."

"Go ahead and reinstate me. You know you're going to do it anyway."

I filled him in on the Lauren Alexander case.

A deputy poked her head into the conference room. "Sheriff, we just got a report of a male trauma patient admitted to the ER with a GSW."

Daniels looked at me with a stern gaze. "Something tells me a few of your bullets may have found their target."

39

It was back to the pale, buzzing fluorescent lights of the emergency room. The sterile, cold air. The smell of disinfectant and latex. The moans and groans. The agonized faces and sad eyes. The whimpers of worried family members. The wet coughs. The bruises and abrasions. The hustle of triage nurses.

I told the receptionist I wanted to speak with Dr. Parker after the suspect was out of surgery.

His name was Heath Chapman. He had priors for DUI, drug possession, and disorderly conduct. In his most recent mugshot, he had long, greasy hair, brown eyes, a narrow face, and a Van Dyke beard. He was late 20s, and according to the records, was 5'10", 167 pounds.

We waited for a little over an hour for the good doctor to emerge. We stood up and greeted him as he exited the double doors that led to the patient rooms.

"I'm getting tired of seeing your faces around here," Parker said.

"It's not my favorite place," I replied in an understated tone.

"You two are here so much you ought to pay rent," Dr. Parker continued. "I can't disclose private health information. But, hypothetically, if a patient sustained a gunshot wound to the lateral portion of his right arm, I'd likely find a proximal humerus fracture, along with a retained bullet in the subacromial space. I would retrieve said bullet, so you would have a good specimen for ballistics."

"Thank you," I said.

"Heath is in a post-op recovery room now. He's a little groggy, but you can talk to him shortly, if you'd like."

I nodded. "Do you know who dropped him off?"

"I'm told that a black SUV dropped him off on the sidewalk. He had lost a lot of blood, but he walked in here on his own."

"I'd like to see that surveillance footage."

"That can be arranged."

Parker escorted us through the double doors to the recovery area. The hallways swarmed with activity. Nurses hustled about. Heart monitors beeped. Doctors were paged over the loudspeaker.

We stepped into the dim recovery room. Privacy curtains separated patients.

Heath looked at us with droopy eyes as we stepped to his bed. IV fluids drained into his arm, and a monitor beside the bed displayed vitals.

"Looks like you're having a rough night," I said.

His eyes filled with concern, recognizing us right away. "I ain't saying shit to you."

I hadn't even flashed my badge yet. He knew who we were.

"Let me tell you how this is going to play out. That bullet they pulled out of your shoulder will be identified as coming from my gun, which I discharged in response to a drive-by shooting earlier this evening. I don't particularly like it when people try to kill me. You're going to go down for attempted murder of a police officer, at the least. And I'm pretty sure I'll be able to connect you to the death of Lauren Alexander and Dylan Reynolds. You're looking at three counts of capital murder. You're never getting out of jail. But there might be some hope for you."

He swallowed hard, and the adrenaline perked him up, despite the residual anesthesia and pain medicine. His heartbeat elevated, and so did his blood pressure. Too much more of this harassment, and I figured a nurse would tell us to leave.

"You tell me who you're working for and who your accomplice was, and maybe you can get a nice deal. You're a young guy. You might be able to breathe free air again someday. It's totally up to you. But that offer's not gonna last long."

He stared at me for a long moment. "I want to talk to an attorney."

"You're not under arrest at the moment. Why would you need an attorney?"

He said nothing.

I'd have to wait until ballistics came back to have probable cause to arrest him. Until then, he was just a victim of a gunshot

"We know Noah Benson hired you. If you testify against him, I'll make sure you see daylight again."

His eyes told me everything I needed to know. We were right on target.

40

"I want it in writing," Heath said.

He wasn't in any condition to agree to anything. To make it ironclad, he would need to be of sound mind, unaffected by anesthesia and pain medication. It would take time to get the state's attorney on board and get the deal done, anyway.

We left the recovery unit and made our way to the trauma ward in the hospital. We strolled through the seafoam green hallways, past pastel seascapes and potted ferns. Ventilators wheezed, and heart monitors blipped. A few nurses scurried about, and doctors did rounds.

I gave a gentle tap on the door before pushing into Mendoza's dim room. He lay in bed with the remote clutched in one hand, watching the flatscreen TV mounted near the ceiling on the wall. His vitals displayed on the monitor bedside the bed, and an IV administered fluids and pain medications.

"How are you feeling?"

"I'm feeling pretty good, all things considered," he said.

"You need anything?"

"To get out of here."

I chuckled.

"The wife just left. I told her to go home and get some rest."

"You will be fit and ready for duty in no time," I said in an optimistic voice.

"I hope so."

"You got lucky."

"If I'd been lucky, I wouldn't have gotten shot."

"True." I paused. "I don't know how much you've heard, but..." I filled him in on the situation with the defective armor.

His face tensed, and his cheeks flushed. After a moment's contemplation, his demeanor changed. "I'm gonna sue those bastards for every dime they've got."

"That's the spirit."

"Tell me you've got something solid."

"We have a few promising leads."

Mendoza grinned. "Shit, boys. When that settlement comes through, I may just retire."

"I hope you get everything you're entitled to."

"Pain and suffering. Emotional distress. Loss of employment. I'm gonna have *fuck you* money."

I laughed. "I hope so."

"And I am not going to be as stupid as you two. You're not going to see me volunteering and giving back to the community. F that."

We laughed.

"Seriously, man. I don't know why you do this. I know we all give each other a lot of shit, but mad props to you guys. If I had a bucket of money, I'd walk away clean."

"I look forward to your retirement party," I said with a grin.

"It's gonna be a doozy."

"We'll let you get your rest. Let us know if you need anything."

We left the hospital and headed back to Diver Down. I called Daniels along the way and filled him in. He said he would talk to the state's attorney.

We stopped in the bar, but the two blondes JD had been talking to earlier had long since vanished. There were plenty more options available.

We hung out, drank our fill, and mingled with the tourists.

Daniels called in the morning. "The slug they pulled out of that punk is a match for your pistol. I'm going to reinstate you and consider that your use of force was justified by the potentially deadly actions of the perpetrators. But try not to shoot people as they're fleeing a crime scene."

"Those were dangerous individuals doing bad things."

"Get to the hospital, arrest Heath, and get a statement that implicates Noah Benson. The OIG can have their fraud case. I want that son-of-a-bitch on conspiracy to commit murder."

"I'm on it."

"I want to put that bastard away for a long time."

"Join the club."

I ended the call and pulled myself out of bed. After I showered and dressed, I stumbled downstairs and banged on the hatch to JD's stateroom.

He groaned.

"We've got bad guys to arrest. Get your ass up!"

I started grilling breakfast in the galley.

After we ate, we stopped by the station, picked up the paperwork, and headed to the hospital. Heath Chapman had been admitted and was ironically on the same floor as Mendoza, two doors down.

JD and I pushed into the punk's room. My jaw clenched when I saw the empty bed.

I checked the bathroom, but he wasn't there.

We rushed into the hallway and talked to the charge nurse.

"Where's the patient that was in unit #303?"

"Your guess is as good as mine," she said. "He must have walked out in the middle of the night."

My face tightened, and I suppressed the urge to grumble a few obscenities under my breath.

41

Daniels put a BOLO out on Heath Chapman. I grabbed my phone and looked up Heath's social media profile. It said he was in a relationship with Wendy Wescott. I figured that was as good a place as any to begin the hunt.

JD and I piled into the Wild Fury van and headed to the *Delphine*. It was a luxury apartment complex with gated under-building parking, modern floor plans, and a few amenities.

I figured we'd do a knock and talk.

We pulled into the visitors' lot, hopped out, and I dialed the property manager from the call box. She buzzed us in, and we took the elevator up to the fifth floor. I banged on the door to unit #516.

I heard commotion inside. Footsteps approached the door. Wendy's timid voice filtered through, "Who is it?"

"Coconut County. Open up."

"Do you have a warrant?"

Her response was a clear indicator we were on target. She didn't need to ask what this was about. She already knew.

"We believe you're harboring a fugitive," I said. "If you don't want me to break down the door, you'll open up."

Heath hissed at her.

I drew my pistol, and so did JD. Suspicion confirmed.

"I'm giving you one last opportunity," I shouted. "If you don't comply, you will go down for aiding and abetting."

Technically, we could breach the premises in pursuit of the fugitive.

"Don't open the fucking door," Heath hissed again at her.

I exchanged a glance with JD.

We were ready to kick the damn thing down when Wendy flipped the deadbolt and pulled the door open.

"What the fuck are you doing!?" Heath shouted.

She stepped aside.

"On the ground, now!" I commanded. "Face down, hands behind your head."

She complied.

We stormed in, weapons drawn.

JD slapped cuffs around Wendy's wrists, and I kept my weapon aimed at Heath. He stood in the living room, looking annoyed. He didn't have anywhere to go, and he sure as hell wasn't going to climb over the balcony and lower himself down. Not in his current condition. His right arm was in a sling.

"What the fuck, man!?"

With Wendy secure, I tossed my cuffs to JD, and he restrained Heath with his hands in front. His shoulder injury precluded cuffing him behind his back, and I didn't figure the county needed a personal injury lawsuit.

I read him his rights and called dispatch to send a patrol unit.

JD escorted him down to the lobby, and I released Wendy.

"I'm not under arrest, am I? I did what you said." Her eyes were wide, and her skin misted with sweat.

"You're not under arrest," I said. "Are you aware of what your boyfriend has been up to?"

She shook her head.

"Well, he tried to kill us last night."

She swallowed hard.

"Before that, we believe he killed two other individuals, Lauren Alexander and Dylan Reynolds. Has he mentioned anything to you?"

She shook her head.

"We have surveillance footage of what we believe is Heath's vehicle running another couple off the road."

Her face tightened.

"He's not a guy you want to be mixed up with. Do yourself a favor and walk away right now. He's going to go away for a long time, with or without your help. But the stronger the case, the better."

She exhaled a deep breath. "He wasn't with me last night. I don't know where he was, but I'm not gonna be his alibi."

"Smart move."

I took a statement from her, gave her my card, and met JD in the lobby.

A patrol car pulled into the visitor lot, and we escorted the perp outside and stuffed him into the backseat.

He moaned and groaned as we shuffled him along. Heath was taken to the station, processed, and printed. We filled out after-action reports in the conference room, then paid him a visit.

We took a seat across the table from Heath and stared him down for a moment.

"This is the part where you start talking," I said.

"What about my deal?"

"That was before you decided to become a pain in the ass."

A hopeless look played on his face. "Come on, man. I just left the hospital. I wasn't under arrest. I was completely free to leave at any time."

"You knew we were coming back for you."

"I'm not clairvoyant. I didn't know what the future would hold."

"Well, you do now. Your future will be spending a long time in a 6x8 cell with an annoying cellmate that has body odor and a penchant for fresh meat."

"I just drove the fucking car. That's all."

"The car that ran Lauren Alexander and Dylan Reynolds off the road."

He frowned.

"Who's your accomplice in this?"

His lips tightened.

"It's not going to be too hard to figure out."

"Justin. Justin Smith," he admitted with a disappointed breath.

I smiled. "See how easy that was? You were hired by Noah Benson. He gave you detonators and det cord to place on the vehicle."

"I don't know the guy. Justin arranged the whole thing. He told me I just had to drive, and I'd get paid. I didn't know what I was getting into."

I regarded him with a healthy dose of skepticism.

42

"When we got too close, Noah had you attempt to take us out," I said.

"I told you, that was Justin's deal," Heath claimed. "He just told me we needed to follow you."

I rolled my eyes. "I suppose you had no idea he was going to attempt to gun us down."

"I mean, yeah, I figured something bad was going to go down."

"Where can we find Justin?"

Heath attempted to shrug but instantly regretted the decision. His face twisted with pain. "Maybe try his apartment."

"Does he have a girlfriend?"

"He sees this girl named Belinda."

"What's her last name?"

"Perkins." His face wrinkled. "How'd you find me?"

"Might want to be careful what you put on social media next time."

Heath grimaced.

"Oh, wait, there's not going to be a next time. My bad."

He frowned at me.

"Have you talked to Justin since he dropped you off at the hospital?"

"No."

I gave him a stern look.

"Okay, yeah, I called him last night after I talked to you guys."

"So, he knows we're looking for him."

"I told him you guys were harassing me. But I promised him I would keep my mouth shut."

"So much for promises," JD snarked. He couldn't help himself.

Heath's brow knitted. "I'm doing you guys a favor."

"And I appreciate it," I said. "You're doing the right thing. Where is Justin now?"

"Maybe I should stop ratting on my friend."

"It's a little late for that."

He glared at me. "If you knew the cops were looking for you, would you go back to your apartment?"

"No."

"It's a good bet he's with Belinda," Heath said.

"Neither one of you really thought this through."

Heath's eyes squinted, annoyed. "I told you—"

"Yeah, yeah, it was all Justin. It will be interesting to see what he has to say about you."

I pushed away from the table and walked to the door.

"Wait! What happens now?" Heath asked. "I told you what you wanted to know. What about my deal?"

"If you continue to cooperate, I'm sure you'll get treated fairly."

"You can't put me in general population. I just ratted on a guy. That's going to get out."

"If you want to be put in protective custody, I'll arrange it. But it's not pretty. No contact with other inmates. You'll be in a small cell 23 hours a day. Lotta people can't hack it."

His face tightened. "Beats getting shanked."

"You got that right."

I knocked on the door, and the guard buzzed us out.

Daniels joined us in the hallway. "Go get his accomplice. Then we're going to take down Noah."

"Any word on Lennox Bradley?" I asked.

"He's still at large. I want all of these clowns behind bars."

The two cases had merged into one.

"By the way," Daniels continued. "Ballistics came back on those Mac-10s found in Lennox's house. One of them matches the slugs pulled from Taylor Knight."

Taylor had been gunned down during a ruthless carjacking. But it was no random act of violence. It was a hit.

Recognition flashed in my eyes. "He and Omar work for Mary Connolly. She was behind the stash house that Shane and Lana knocked off."

"Looks that way. Find Lennox and make something stick on Connolly."

"With pleasure."

We stopped by the main office and visited with Denise. She looked up Belinda Perkins's address. With Heath's statement, we were able to get a warrant for Justin. We readied another tactical team and headed to her apartment. She lived in the *Atlantis*. It was another luxury mid-rise with under-building parking and nice amenities.

We pulled into the visitor parking lot, followed by Erickson and Faulkner. I figured that was enough to handle the situation.

We hopped out of the van and hustled to the main entrance. JD caught the door as a young blonde strutted out. She was distracting. We all had to take a glance before continuing into the lobby.

Jack pressed the call button, and we waited on the elevator. This time, we were decked out in full tactical gear with vests that weren't manufactured by ARMG Unlimited.

The door slid open, and we piled in. The elevator took us up to the third floor, and we flooded into the hallway and advanced to unit #309.

I banged a heavy fist against the door and shouted, "Coconut County! We have a warrant!"

Commotion stirred inside.

I nodded to Erickson and Faulkner.

They heaved a battering ram against the door. It took two hits to smash through the deadbolt, twisting the steel jam. The door flung open, and I tossed a flash-bang grenade down the foyer.

It clattered against the tile, then bounced onto the hardwoods in the living room.

We hovered in the hallway, and I plugged my ears and closed my eyes as the deafening bang reverberated, filling the room with haze.

I swung the barrel of my pistol into the apartment, and we advanced down the foyer, clearing the kitchen to the left.

Belinda shrieked in horror as we pushed through the soupy haze.

Justin had darted through the sliding glass doors onto the balcony. As an able-bodied young man, he was able to scale the railing and lower himself down.

I rushed onto the terrace and angled my weapon over the railing at him. "Stop right there!"

He looked up at me with tense brown eyes. Justin was a beefy guy in his late 20s with short brown hair, a thick beard, and a puffy face. He looked like he was on the juice and retaining a little water weight.

He didn't heed my command.

Justin kept descending, but in his hurried pace, he didn't think things through. He lost his grip and fell away. He smacked the railing below, sending him cartwheeling toward the ground.

The fall seemed to happen in slow motion.

I winced, anticipating the ugliness of the splat.

Justin tumbled end-over-end but somehow managed to land on his feet momentarily before tumbling to break the fall. The stainless steel pistol tucked in his waistband crashed to the concrete in the alley behind the apartment building. Justin tried to get up, but his ankle was at a 90° angle. The crack sounded like a twig snapping.

Justin grabbed the gun and tried to stagger away, but it wasn't working.

Faulkner and Erickson raced out of the apartment.

I followed.

JD stayed behind to keep an eye on things.

The deputies sprinted down the hallway, pushed into the stairwell, and spiraled down. Footsteps clattered off the steel steps, ringing in the stairwell.

They burst into the hallway, then pushed through an emergency exit into the alley behind the building.

I followed them outside as they sprinted toward Justin as he hopped away.

"Freeze!" Erickson shouted, his weapon drawn.

43

Justin did the dumb thing and aimed the pistol in our direction. He squeezed off a few shots.

The deafening bang echoed in the alleyway.

It sounded like a .45 ACP.

Copper rounds snapped through the air.

We all returned fire and ducked for cover, but there wasn't much.

Bullets crisscrossed the alleyway.

Justin was a good 40 yards away, and in the heat of the moment, nobody hit anything.

The whole thing probably lasted 15 or 20 seconds but felt like 10 minutes. Justin hobbled in the middle of the alley, unloading the magazine at us.

Three times as many bullets came back in his direction.

I needed the guy alive.

A cartridge jammed the ejection port of Justin's pistol.

He tossed the weapon down and raised his hands in the air, realizing he was screwed. "Alright, alright. I give up."

The sharp scent of gunpowder lingered in the air.

We advanced down the alley, keeping our weapons aimed at him.

"Down on the ground!" Faulkner shouted. "Now!"

Justin hobbled to the ground, ate the pavement, and put his hands behind his head. He knew the drill. This wasn't the first time he'd been arrested.

Erickson kicked the perp's pistol away, keeping his gun aimed at the suspect. Faulkner slapped the cuffs around his wrists, and Justin groaned, every movement aggravating his broken ankle.

I called for an ambulance. The meat wagon arrived 15 minutes later, red lights flickering.

Faulkner read Justin his rights, and the EMTs attended to his injury. He was transferred to a gurney, loaded into the back of the ambulance, and whisked away.

JD watched the whole thing from the balcony above with a grin on his face. He displayed a black Uzi, dangling from his gloved hand. "Look what I found!"

We returned to the apartment. Belinda sat on the sofa, looking distraught.

"How much do you want to bet ballistics on this match the slugs pulled from the walls at Dunsel?" JD said.

There was no doubt in my mind.

We interrogated Belinda. She maintained the position that she was unaware of Justin's activities and didn't know he was a fugitive.

There was a small tray of weed on the coffee table. Upon searching the rest of the apartment, we found an eight-ball of cocaine in a dresser drawer. We arrested Belinda for possession and brought her down to the station. I figured it might give us some leverage if she knew information about Justin's crimes. She might be willing to talk if it meant dropping the charges.

Justin was taken to the emergency room and triaged. He was already in a patient room by the time we arrived. We'd been in there so much we were on a first-name basis with the receptionist. I told her I wanted to speak with the perp as soon as possible.

Once they got him fixed up, we had a chat with him. Justin's ankle was in a cast, and the minor abrasions on his hands and elbows had been bandaged.

He scowled at us as we entered the room. "I ain't saying nothing to you."

"I don't blame you. It would normally be in your best interest to shut the hell up. But with Heath willing to testify, we don't really need anything from you."

His face tightened.

"We recovered your Uzi from your girlfriend's apartment. How much do you want to bet the ballistics from that weapon match the slugs from your little drive-by at Dunsel?"

His cheeks reddened, and concern filled his eyes.

"Heath already told us that you were the one in contact with Noah."

The muscles in his jaw flexed.

"How much dirty work have you done for Noah?"

Justin said nothing.

"We found a prepaid cellular in your pocket when you were arrested. I wonder if we will be able to tie that phone to Noah Benson? I wonder how many times you guys talked about murdering people?"

The wheels turned behind his eyes.

"Not that you care, but a deputy almost died because of Noah's malfeasance. He's not a good dude, and he put a lot of people at risk. Who knows how many other people are out there, relying on his products to keep them safe?" I paused. "See, I'm pretty pissed off about the fact that you tried to kill us. But I'm more pissed off that a friend and colleague is still in this very hospital and will be for quite some time. So, I don't care as much about you as I do Noah Benson. You hand him to me, and I'm sure the state's attorney will reward your cooperation."

"I want to talk to a lawyer."

I tried to hide my displeasure.

That was the end of the conversation. We had to stop interviewing him.

We left the emergency room and stepped outside. The fresh air smelled good after the antiseptic atmosphere of the hospital.

We hopped into the van and headed to Oyster Avenue to grab lunch. People were nursing hangovers from the night before, but it was still crowded. Nothing like the night, but busy enough.

College students wondered about like drunken zombies, hopping from bar to bar, testing their endurance. There were already casualties of war, and I saw more than one girl hurling in an alleyway.

It had been a hell of a morning, and we were ready to unwind. We stopped in the Coconut Grill, and the hostess seated us in a high-backed cherry wood booth. The restaurant had that classic, upscale feel with white mosaic tile and black accents. There was a full bar, a large flatscreen, and fixed stools. You could get a little of everything at the Coconut Grill. The milkshakes and sundaes were sinful.

We browsed the menu, and it wasn't long before a delightful strawberry blonde stopped by the table with a cheery welcome. "Afternoon, boys. I'm Camdyn. I'll be serving you today. Are you ready to order, or do you need more time?"

JD and I exchanged a nod.

"I think we know what we want," JD said.

Jack ordered the Caribbean BBQ Shrimp, and I went with a cheeseburger.

Camdyn scribbled on her pad, collected the menus with a smile, and darted away.

My phone buzzed with a call from Isabella as we waited for the meal to arrive. "I've been scanning the luxury rentals on Arcadia Cay, filtering by price," Isabella said. "A couple recently rented a villa. The timing coincides with Skyler's kidnapping. Looks like they arranged it a few days before. It's one of the pricier options on the island at $6,000 a day."

"That's nothing if you're a new billionaire," I said.

"I called the property owner, inquiring about the next availability. It's a 12-bedroom, 20,000-square-foot mansion on the beach. They told me they didn't know when the property would next be available. The current tenant is paying cash, well over market. I fished a little and discovered it was a young couple in their mid-to-late 20s. The description possibly matches Skyler and her bodyguard. But from what the owner said, the woman is a brunette with short hair. Doesn't surprise me that Skyler would change her appearance." Isabella paused. "I've got a plan if you're up for it."

"You sound determined," I said.

"I am. A lot of people lost everything. We're going to get that money back."

"Let's hear your plan."

44

A sleek *Slipstream G-750* waited for us on the tarmac at the FBO. The polished fuselage glimmered in the Florida sun. With space-age technology and an elegant design, it was the premier jet for private travel. Isabella had arranged it for us. She was serious about recovering the funds.

Denise took a few vacation days and joined the adventure. Of course, she told Sheriff Daniels she was going somewhere else with a girlfriend. I don't think he would have approved of our taking her on one of our crazy unsanctioned missions. I planned on keeping her out of harm's way. But, you know what they say about plans…

We boarded the luxury aircraft and were greeted by the flight crew. The interior smelled like a mix of jet exhaust and fine leather. We slipped into the supple seats and relaxed. Cabin attendants catered to our every need.

"Is this how you guys always travel?" Denise asked, taking in the impressive accommodations.

JD grinned. "Perks of the job."

"I don't get these kinds of perks."

"You're getting them now."

I buckled my seatbelt and reclined my chair. A delightful blonde flight attendant took my drink order.

Another attendant pulled the cabin door shut, and the captain's voice crackled over the intercom a few moments later. "We'll begin taxiing toward the runway soon. We should be wheels up shortly. I'm expecting clear skies today, and we should have you at your destination in just over an hour. Sit back, relax, and enjoy the flight. Don't hesitate to let us know if there's anything we can do to make your trip more enjoyable."

Once we were cleared for takeoff, the engines whined, and the aircraft raced down the tarmac, picking up speed. The scenery whizzed by, and soon, the nose lifted. The craft rocketed skyward, and the pilot retracted the landing gear with a clunk as we ascended toward the pillowy clouds.

I sunk into my seat and nodded off until the wheels screeched down at the FBO in Arcadia Cay.

We'd left our weapons behind. This was a snatch-and-grab —in and out without a hitch. Or so, that was the plan. The local authorities didn't much care for foreigners bringing in weapons. Despite the touristy nature of the island paradise, crime was high. Guns were involved in over 60% of local crimes. Most of the weapons used were trafficked from the United States. We didn't need any trouble. We were asking for enough.

Isabella had arranged transportation, and a car picked us up on the tarmac and drove us to the upscale neighborhood of Paradise Cove. The driver headed east on JFK. It took a minute for my brain to adjust to racing down the road on the wrong side, especially since our car was a left-hand drive vehicle. Most are imported from the States.

Traffic laws were more of a suggestion on the island, and our driver acted like this was a Formula One race.

Surrounded by turquoise water, the island lived up to its reputation as a tropical paradise. We weaved through the streets and passed expansive resorts and restaurants to a villa near the golf course.

Isabella had rented an estate not far from the target's house on a secluded drive with no outlet. I didn't ask what she paid for it, but it wasn't cheap. Not quite as opulent as the home our suspects had rented, but nothing to sneeze at.

The two-story estate had a cobblestone drive, mauve stucco walls, and an orange Spanish tile roof.

The property manager greeted us as we pulled into the driveway. Our driver parked near the main entrance and killed the engine. He hopped out, got our doors, and attended to the baggage.

We climbed out, and Patsy introduced herself. She was a pear-shaped woman with short auburn hair and too much makeup. "Welcome to Arcadia Cay. I hope you had a good journey."

"Thank you," JD said. "We did."

"Let me show you around the property."

She escorted us to the main entrance, and the driver helped with the luggage, though we didn't have much. Denise packed light.

We climbed the steps to the portico with grand columns and archways.

JD gave the driver a nice tip after he set the bags in the foyer. Then he was off to his next fare.

The mansion exuded luxury and splendor. Detailed craftsmanship at every turn. Marble tile with intricate inlays, custom millwork, elevator access, and hurricane-rated doors and windows. In the living room, there was a coffered ceiling and a set of bay windows that offered a stunning view of the infinity pool and the teal water beyond. There was a hot tub and access to a private beach.

Denise's eyes filled with wonder as she marveled at the grand structure. "Not too shabby."

"It will do," JD said in a sardonic voice.

Patsy gave us a tour of the various bedrooms and living areas. There was a rec room with a pool table and dart boards. A workout room. A dry sauna.

Denise claimed the room with lavender walls and louvered shutters on the windows. A white, four-post bed was the centerpiece. The room had a soft, cozy vibe.

Tall palms swayed in the breeze, guarding the tropical oasis. The house seemed to go on forever. Well-decorated rooms, fine art, elegant appointments, luxury bathrooms. It was a place that instantly made you feel at ease. The kind of place you could get used to and never want to leave. It was almost too bad we were here to work.

Patsy gave us two sets of keys and bid us farewell.

JD and I picked out our rooms and got settled in, then we all regrouped in the living room.

Denise had already changed into a bikini. With a towel in hand and a bottle of lotion, she was ready for an afternoon of poolside bliss.

JD and I tried not to stare at her delightful figure.

We failed miserably.

The luscious redhead was a vision, and that tiny bikini was a far cry from the polyester uniform. With a wide-brimmed hat and sunglasses, she smiled and said, "I don't know about you boys, but I'm officially on vacation. How about one of you fix me a margarita?"

It took a few moments before my brain could formulate a response. I was too distracted by the taut fabric. *Oh, to be a thread of 100% cotton.*

"One margarita, coming right up," JD said with a grin.

He strutted to the wet bar that was stocked with every imaginable brand of premium liquor. There were packets of mixes for margaritas, daiquiris, piña coladas, and other tropical drinks. The owner had anticipated every desire.

Jacked grabbed a bottle of tequila, triple sec, and a secret ingredient that I can't reveal. He snagged a packet of margarita mix and dumped the ingredients, along with a scoop of ice from the machine, into an industrial-strength stainless steel blender. The blades swirled, and the motor howled as he mixed the concoction, dicing the ice into a fine consistency. He rimmed the glass with salt, affixed a lime, then poured in the thick and slushy green margarita. With a pleasant smile, he delivered it to the fiery beauty. "Here you go, dear!"

Her delicate hands took the glass, and I grabbed the door for her as she sauntered onto the patio and made herself at home on a lounge chair by the pool.

"You let me know if you need any help applying that lotion," I said.

"I think I've got it covered, thank you," she replied with a smirk, knowing exactly what effect she had on me.

JD muttered in my ear. "I'd like to get that uncovered."

I gave him a look. "We're here to work."

"You ought to work on that."

45

Despite my urge to abandon the mission and attend to Denise's suntan, JD and I decided to recon the targets. We went for a leisurely stroll down the private beach that served dozens of luxury homes. The turquoise water sparkled, and waves crashed against the shore. We carried colorful beach towels, wore sunglasses, and a camera dangled from my neck. We tried to look like typical tourists.

A gorgeous woman with short raven hair strutted toward us, her feet sinking into the sand with each step. She paid us no attention. Her eyes were focused on the soothing water and frothy surf. A cream bikini accented her tan skin, svelte form, and natural endowments.

I almost didn't recognize her, but the pistol tattoos on her tummy just inside her pelvis were a dead giveaway. I recognized them from pictures on Skyler's Instabook feed.

With my camera on silent shutter, I snapped several inconspicuous photos as she approached. It was Skyler Graham, alright. There was no doubt about it.

She marched past us, and we pretended not to notice.

We continued down the beach to the villa she was renting. Like most of the homes in this area, there was a large patio with a pool. A short path through the trimmed hedges led to the beach.

I looked through the floor-to-ceiling windows of the estate but didn't see anyone else inside.

I told JD to pose for a picture, his back to the water.

I backed away, pretending to frame up the shot. I kept working my way closer to the villa. A low perimeter wall surrounded the property.

I backed to the access gate, still pretending to photograph JD. My hand fumbled with the knob. The gate was unlocked.

From my pocket, I dug out a small spycam and peeled off the adhesive backing. I placed the wireless device inside the gate on one of the wrought iron bars. The tiny black cam, the size of a button, blended in. The ultra-HD sensor would give a clear view of the patio and the living room.

I walked back down the beach and rejoined JD. I launched an app on my phone and connected to the cellular-enabled spycam that served as its own mobile hotspot.

We were able to see a clear picture as we walked back toward our villa. I sent Isabella the snaps of Skyler and shared access to the camera feed.

Target confirmed.

She called me a moment later. The glee in her voice was apparent. "I knew it."

"What now?"

"Keep tabs on the house. When she leaves, get inside. The funds were transferred from the XTC exchange to a crypto wallet. Those funds have not moved from that wallet, except for a slight amount that would account for their living expenses. Nobody leaves that kind of money in a software wallet—too risky. It has to be on a hardware wallet."

Cryptocurrencies could be stored online in software wallets or offline in a hardware wallet. The hardware wallet was a much safer option. It could be disconnected from the Internet. Anything online was vulnerable to attacks.

The hardware wallet was useless without the pin and passcode. A 12- or 24-word seed phrase gave the user the ability to recover the wallet on a new device if the original was lost or stolen.

"I'm betting they've got the hardware wallet in their possession," Isabella said. "Find it, and figure out her pin and passcode. As we discussed, it's most likely in the safe."

When Isabella had talked to the property owner, she mentioned the need for storing jewelry if she rented the villa in the future. The owner assured her the estate had a safe for valuables and went so far as to tell her the brand and model. It's amazing the information people will tell you when trying to make a sale.

"Getting into the house is the easy part," I said. "Getting into the safe and figuring out the access codes could prove difficult."

"She may have her passcodes and seed phrases memorized, but I guarantee it's written down somewhere. You don't chance that amount of money to memory. Find the codes, and we will have access to all the funds and can transfer them out of the wallet."

"Easier said than done."

"I have faith in you."

"I appreciate the confidence."

I ended the call, and we returned to our villa.

Denise was still lounging poolside, her margarita glass perilously close to empty. "Did you have a nice walk?"

"We did," I said with a smile.

She lifted her glass with perfectly manicured fingers and wiggled it. "I'm empty. Fill me."

She knew exactly how loaded the statement was.

I took her glass and stepped inside. There was still a good amount left in the blender. I refilled the glass and returned it to her while JD hustled down the street and placed another spycam on the mailbox across the street from the target's estate. He got brave and put a GPS tracker on the red convertible Mustang that was in the driveway.

I set the devices to send motion alerts anytime they picked up movement. My phone would buzz with an alert every time somebody walked by, but it would keep us from missing the suspects if they stepped out.

"You're never going to believe this," JD said when he returned. He had a tormented look on his face.

"What?"

"Veronica or Vanessa, or whatever she's calling herself now, is here."

"What!?"

"Yup. Looks like she's renting a villa down the street. Probably using a fake name and somebody else's funds."

"That girl gets around. Did she see you?"

"I don't think so."

"She's not the priority here."

JD's face wrinkled. "She set me on fire!"

"Not the priority. Let's keep focused. We complete the mission first. Then we can worry about her."

We hung out for the rest of the afternoon, and Denise soaked up the sun, along with a few margaritas. Maybe a few too many.

Since we were on a glorified stakeout, Jack ordered pizza. It took over an hour to arrive. I'm not sure what the delay was. On an island this size, it should have gotten here a lot faster, but nobody seemed to be in a hurry on the island.

Nevertheless, it was gooey, tangy, and tasty.

With a head full of tequila, Denise ate a few slices, then took a power nap. *Passed out* would be a more appropriate way to describe it.

After getting dozens of motion alerts from the wireless cameras, none of which were our subjects, I finally got one that sparked my interest.

JD huddled over my phone as we watched the screen. Skyler and Maverick, who'd also cut and dyed his hair, hopped into the red Mustang convertible and pulled out of the driveway.

"Looks like they're going out," JD said. "Now's as good a time as any. They're probably going to dinner. I'm guessing we've got at least an hour."

"Longer with the time it takes to get served around here."

I grabbed a baseball cap and sunglasses and shouldered a small backpack full of goodies.

JD tucked his hair under a hat and ditched his loud Hawaiian shirt, going into incognito mode.

We looked like we were up to no good as we pushed onto the patio and took the path to the beach. I glanced around as we hustled down to Skyler's estate. I saw a few neighbors inside their homes and a couple strolling the beach, hand in hand.

The amber sun dipped toward the horizon, painting the sky in various shades of pink and blue. It was a beautiful evening.

At the gate to Skyler's villa, I gave another look around. When it was clear, we both donned surgical masks to cover our faces in case of surveillance cameras.

Skyler had left the gate unlocked.

We pulled on gloves, slipped into the backyard, crossed the patio, and rounded the pool. I pulled on a pair of gloves and climbed the latticework to the terrace that overlooked the backyard. JD followed as I scaled the balustrade.

The terrace door was locked, but I didn't see any alarm sensors or wiring. Usually, only first-floor windows and doors were wired.

JD knelt down, pulled out a lock-picking kit from his wallet, and fiddled with the mechanism. It was a standard pin and tumbler design. Within a few seconds, he twisted the handle and opened the door. He proudly motioned for me to enter. "After you."

My eyes scanned the bedroom as I stepped inside.

I didn't think anyone else was at home, and I hadn't seen or heard any dogs.

We began rummaging through the place. It was massive. Twice the size of the house we were staying in. But there are only so many rooms a person can occupy. We found a laptop on a desk in the master bedroom.

In the walk-in closet that was bigger than my first apartment, we found the personal safe. It had keypad access, and was the size of a small microwave. Built like a tank with thick carbon steel, it was heavy and bulky. Though it wasn't bolted down, it wasn't something you wanted to lug down the street.

I pulled out my phone, attached a high-end infrared camera, and visualized the keypad. This wasn't a store-bought device. It was an advanced unit that could distinguish micro fluctuations in temperature. But even with this device, in the 10 minutes it took to hustle down the beach and break into the villa, there were only faint thermal variations where numbers had been recently pressed. Soon, they would be the temperature of all the other keys. Indistinguishable.

I could barely make out a four-digit code. The thermal differences between the other numbers on the keypad faded away quickly. It was impossible to discern the order they had been pressed.

Skyler must have accessed the safe before she left for dinner. Hell, if I had $40 billion stashed in a safe, I'd check it frequently, too.

JD launched the tracking app on his phone and monitored the red Mustang. "Looks like they drove to a restaurant on the east side."

I texted Isabella and asked her to look up Skyler's birthday.

Isabella texted me back a moment later, and I punched in the month and the day.

It didn't open the safe.

There were a limited number of options at this point. I kept trying logical permutations of the four-digit code, but nothing worked. There were only 256 possible variations, so I'd get there, eventually, but I didn't want to do this the hard way.

I texted her again: [What about Owen Patterson?]

Isabella responded a moment later. The first four digits of his birthday was a potential match. I punched in the code, but it didn't work.

46

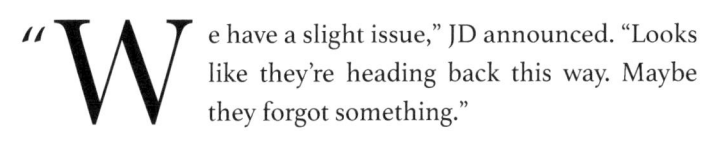

"We have a slight issue," JD announced. "Looks like they're heading back this way. Maybe they forgot something."

"What do we have, 15 minutes?"

"If that."

I tried reversing the order of the digits, and the safe unlocked.

"That's cold," JD said. "The girl steals his fortune, drives him to suicide, and uses a variation of his birthday as her safe code? I bet it's her phone's password, too. Ruthless."

I pulled open the safe.

Inside was a single hardware wallet the size of a USB drive. Along with it, a folded scrap of paper with 24 random words scribbled on it, a four-digit PIN number that was identical to the safe code, and a passphrase.

It was bad security protocol to keep everything in the same place and to reuse PIN numbers, but people get lazy. On the flip side, there were people with millions stuck in a crypto wallet that they couldn't access because they lost their password, PIN, or seed phrase.

The perils of self-custody.

You didn't technically need the hardware wallet if you had the seed phrase. You could restore the wallet to a new device, provided you had the proper 12 or 24 words.

A thud in another room drew my attention.

JD and I exchanged a concerned glance. He looked at the tracking app on his phone and whispered, "They're not even halfway here."

I took both the wallet and the paper, then closed the safe. I slipped the paper into my back pocket.

We stepped out of the walk-in closet and were greeted by twitchy barrels of semi-automatic pistols held by two thugs, their faces covered by bandannas.

It seemed we weren't the only ones who had the idea to rip off Skyler Graham.

I suspected she had been flaunting her wealth around town, and somebody else may have figured out who she was. Perhaps these goons randomly decided to knock off a luxury home.

That thought was put to rest when one of the dickheads said, "Hand over the wallet."

The barrel of his pistol stared me down as I contemplated my next move.

47

I tossed the hardware wallet to the big thug. His eyes were distracted by the device as it tumbled through the air.

The goons were too far away for us to make a move.

The Big Guy caught the device and bobbled it. He tried to save it as it bounced around his fingertips. It eluded his grasp and clattered against the tile. He knelt down, keeping his eyes and the gun aimed at me while his buddy covered Jack.

The Big Guy snatched the wallet and stood up. "What's the PIN?"

"How should I know?" I said.

"Don't fuck with me, man. What's the PIN?"

"I. Don't. Know. The wallet was the only thing in the safe."

"How did you get into the safe?"

"Lucky guess."

"What was the lucky guess?"

"Do you really think someone's gonna be stupid enough to keep the same PIN on their safe as they do on their hardware wallet?" I knew many were.

"Tell me the PIN, or I'll blow your fucking head off."

He marched toward me, sticking the barrel of the gun in my face. The scent of gun oil hit my nose.

I struck across in the blink of an eye, grabbing the barrel, shoving it toward the ceiling.

The thug squeezed the trigger, and the deafening bang filled the room.

Muzzle flash flickered, and smoke drifted from the barrel.

I struck across with my other hand, smacking his forearm, twisting the pistol around, stripping the weapon.

His comrade squeezed off a shot but hit the Big Guy.

Blood erupted from the man's back, and the bullet exited through his chest, missing me by inches.

The thug flopped to the ground, soaking the tile with blood.

I returned fire and put two into his partner's chest.

The goon tumbled back and fell against the dresser. He slid to the ground, leaving a streak of blood on the wood.

The scent of gunpowder lingered, and my ears rang.

I looked at JD. "You alright?"

He nodded. "So much for in and out without a hitch."

My body vibrated with adrenaline.

There was no explaining this to the local authorities. We were out of our jurisdiction and had broken into someone's house. We were in the process of stealing $40 billion worth of cryptocurrency. There was no way we were going to talk our way out of this one.

I placed the gun in the Big Guy's dead hand. I'd been wearing gloves and wasn't concerned about prints.

JD and I left the stiffs, hustled onto the terrace, and climbed back down the way we came. The sun had long since vanished over the horizon, and the sky was midnight blue.

The neighbors, if they were home, had to hear the gunshots.

We crouched low, hustling across the patio to the back gate. We pushed through and raced down the beach, then cut between the houses. I didn't want witnesses to see us return to our villa.

The street was empty when we crossed. We darted between more houses, then found ourselves on the golf course.

I called Isabella as we took cover behind some shrubs. "We need immediate exfiltration."

"You sound stressed. What happened?"

"Small SNAFU. Someone else had their sights on the wallet."

"I'll see what I can do."

We ditched the hats and masks, changed our shirts to ones I had in my backpack, then circled around and returned to the villa like we had been out for a leisurely stroll.

I hurried inside, climbed the steps, and found Denise still asleep in her lavender room. I gently shook her shoulder. "Wake up, sleepyhead. We're leaving."

She peeled open groggy eyes. "What?"

"Vacation's over. We're going back to Coconut Key."

"Why?"

"Mission accomplished. Sort of. No time to explain. Get your things together. We're leaving now."

She pulled herself out of bed, and I hustled to my room, opened my laptop at the desk, and plugged in the hardware wallet. I accessed the device, punched in the PIN code, and gained access to the main wallet.

There was only one Bitcoin.

One!

I was sure there was a hidden wallet. You could create them by entering a passphrase. If you typed the right phrase, it would take you to the hidden wallet. If you typed the wrong phrase, it would create a new hidden wallet.

I entered the passphrase written on the paper.

Sure enough, that gave me access to the full $40 billion worth of crypto.

I breathed a relieved sigh.

JD grabbed his things and stepped into the room. "We need to roll. What's the plan?"

"Isabella said she's sending a car."

I transferred the entire amount to Isabella's crypto wallet address, then disconnected the device. I tossed it in the trash. It was useless at this point. I closed my computer, and stuffed it into my backpack. I shouldered it, grabbed my go bag, and we hustled out of the room.

I rushed to check on Denise. She was still gathering her things.

"Train is leaving. Now! We need to go."

"What happened?"

"It's better if you don't ask."

She gave me a suspicious look.

Denise finished stuffing her bag. I grabbed it once it was zippered shut, and we hurried downstairs and waited in the foyer for a car to arrive.

48

A cab pulled into the driveway.

We darted outside, and I tossed our luggage into the trunk. The three of us crammed into the backseat, and I told the driver, "Get us to the airport in 20 minutes, and there's an extra hundred in it for you."

He had the car in reverse, screeching out of the driveway before I finished. We flew into the street, and the driver dropped it into gear. The tires barked as he launched forward. We blazed down the residential street, racing past sprawling mansions.

Two police cars screeched around the corner, blocking our path.

Our driver jammed the brakes.

We lurched forward as the car slowed, and the nose dived.

The officers hopped out of their cars and drew their weapons, taking aim at us. There were four of them.

"So much for getting to the airport," JD grumbled.

"Out of the car, now!" the sergeant shouted.

"There's a thousand in it for you if you can get us out of this one," JD said to the driver.

He thought about it for a moment, the engine still running.

"Too much trouble," he said.

He put the car in park, killed the engine, and slowly opened the door. He stepped out with his hands in the air. "I'm just the driver."

The officers waved him away, and he stepped onto the lawn.

"What did you guys do?" Denise asked.

"Everybody play it cool," I said. "This is all gonna work out fine."

Nobody believed me. I didn't believe me either.

"Step out of the vehicle!" the sergeant shouted.

I pulled the lever and opened the door. I stepped out with my hands in the air.

JD and Denise followed.

"On the ground," the sergeant commanded. "Face down. Now!"

We weren't used to being on this end of it.

We complied and ate the pavement that was still warm from a full day of tropical sun.

Next thing I knew, hard steel slapped around my wrists. I was cuffed behind my back. Two officers struggled to lift me to my feet. They shoved me against a patrol car with my companions.

"Can I go now?" the driver asked. "I have another fare."

The sergeant stared him down for a moment and said nothing.

Another officer patted me down and took my wallet, keys, and money clip. He found my badge and seemed amused. "You have no jurisdiction here, my friend."

My money found its way into his pocket.

He moved over and groped Denise.

"Hey, watch it, buddy!" she growled as he cupped a handful of her pert bottom.

My jaw tightened, and my blood boiled.

They confiscated JD's and Denise's personal belongings as well.

The sergeant questioned the driver. "Where are you taking these people?"

"The airport."

"Did they give you anything?"

"No."

"Do you know these people?"

"No."

"Have you driven for them before?"

"No."

"Empty your pockets."

His jaw tightened, but he complied. He pulled out his keys and his phone, and some cash.

The sergeant held out his hand, and the driver glared at him. He knew what was happening.

The sergeant continued to hold out his hand until the driver put the money in it. The bills quickly vanished into the sergeant's pocket.

"Your wallet and ID," the sergeant said.

The driver pulled it out and handed it to him with an angry face.

The sergeant looked over the ID, took a few bills that were in the wallet, then handed it back to the man. "Get out of here. Leave their baggage."

The driver hustled back to the car, popped the trunk, and tossed our bags onto the road. He slammed the trunk lid, hopped into the vehicle, and started it up. Another officer moved his patrol car out of the way, and the taxi zipped away into the night.

"Why are we being detained?" I asked.

An officer looked at me and said nothing.

They stuffed us into the back of patrol cars, drove down the street, and pulled into the driveway of the villa that Skyler had rented. Denise and I were in the back of one car, and JD was in the back of another.

The red Mustang was parked near the entrance. Skyler and Maverick waited in the open doorway.

"I don't need to tell you that you're in big trouble," the sergeant said to me, glancing in the rearview.

I played dumb. "I don't know what you're talking about. We're here on vacation."

He popped the trunk, climbed out of the car, and grabbed our bags. He lugged them to the front door, and there was a brief exchange with Skyler. He carried the bags inside. I assumed they were going to search the contents.

Denise and I were alone in the back of the patrol car.

"I don't like this, Tyson."

"I don't like it either."

"This looks serious."

"It is."

"What happened?" she hissed again.

"You don't want to know."

The uneasy sensation in my gut tightened. The medical examiner wasn't on the scene. There were no emergency medical responders. No forensic team.

The sergeant returned to the patrol car, opened the door, and pulled Denise out. He escorted her inside, and she gave a worried glance at me over her shoulder before disappearing.

My jaw tightened again.

I looked at JD in the patrol car behind me. He fidgeted, trying to find a way out of the cuffs.

I didn't have anything to pick the lock with, and neither did he. They'd taken everything from our pockets. I could try to kick the window out, but I didn't think I'd get far. Two officers remained outside, keeping watch.

They kept Denise in the house for at least 15 minutes, probably interrogating her. It was a standard tactic to separate suspects and interview them individually. Easier to get them to flip on one another.

These particular officers didn't seem aboveboard, either. And I was a little concerned about their idea of justice.

The sergeant emerged from the house and marched to the patrol car. He pulled open the door and ordered me out. I complied, and he grabbed my arm and marched me into the house.

I still didn't see Denise.

As I had suspected, all of our luggage had been gone through. The suitcases were open on the floor, and the contents scattered across the tile in the foyer. My laptop was out, and an officer was trying to get past the security screen.

Skyler glared at me. "Where is it?"

"Where is what?" I asked.

Rage filled her eyes, her teeth gnashed, and the veins in her neck bulged. In a slow growl, she asked, "Where. Is. It?"

"I don't know what you're talking about."

"Bullshit!"

She glared at me for another moment, and I said nothing.

"There are two dead guys in my bedroom, and my safe has been broken into."

"That's terrible. What does that have to do with me?"

"You think I'm playing a fucking game with you? Do you have any idea what I'm capable of?"

Her cold eyes stared into me. I had a pretty good idea of what she was capable of.

She pulled out her cell phone and displayed surveillance footage from the bedroom. There we were, in full high-definition. Our little second story act and the confrontation with the two thugs. Sure, JD and I both wore hats, glasses, and masks, but there was no hiding our physical shapes.

Still, I chose to deny it. "What's that?"

Skyler's hateful eyes narrowed. "Keep playing dumb, asshole. See where that gets you." She was on the verge of exploding. Skyler took a deep breath and calmed herself. "I want the hardware wallet and the passcodes. Do I need to spell out what's going to happen if I don't get them back?"

I began to realize these officers weren't here in an official capacity. They were most likely on Skyler's payroll. Something told me we were all at risk of disappearing.

49

The sergeant moved me into the living room, and the two from outside joined.

Another officer pulled Denise in a few moments later. Her terrified eyes flicked to me.

An officer put a gun to her head.

My heart leapt into my throat.

"Tell me where the wallet is, or this is going to get messy," Skyler demanded.

It was already messy.

I said to the officers, "You guys really haven't thought this through, have you?"

"You're the one who hasn't thought this through," Skyler snapped.

"How is Skyler going to pay you when she doesn't have any money?" I asked the dirty cops.

The officers exchanged wary glances.

"What are you talking about?"

"The crypto. It's gone. Poof. All of it. It's been transferred out of your wallet."

Her face reddened, and she looked like she was about to burst. "I want it back, now!"

"So, you're admitting you're broke."

Her jaw tightened.

"No money to pay for this rental," I said. "Nothing to pay your henchmen."

There were more nervous glances among the officers.

"We want our funds now," the sergeant said.

"She doesn't have it," I said. "Please tell me you at least got half up front."

Skyler tried to remain calm. "I can assure you, gentlemen, you will get paid the minute I recover that wallet."

"So it's true? You no longer have the funds."

"They're mine. They belong to me. And this asshole will return them, or his girlfriend is going to die."

"I'm not his girlfriend," Denise muttered.

"Shut up."

"What's she paying you?" I asked.

The officers exchanged a glance.

"100,000 each," the sergeant said.

I scoffed. "Is that all? I'll double it right now. Let us go, and take her into custody."

"What about the bodies upstairs? It will be an extra fee to take care of that."

"You aren't seriously considering this, are you?" Skyler asked.

The sergeant shrugged.

"Maverick, do something!" Skyler exclaimed, paranoia and panic swelling.

Maverick hesitated, then moved his hand toward his pistol, holstered in his waistband.

BANG!

The sergeant shot him before he had a chance to draw his weapon. The thundering boomed echoed, and blood erupted from Maverick's chest. He tumbled back against the wall, then slid down, streaking the beige paint with fresh crimson.

Skyler shrieked, and her body trembled. She swallowed her fear and tried to remain calm. She spoke in a slow, deliberate manner, trying to keep an optimistic tone. "I can see we need to renegotiate our terms."

"But you have nothing to negotiate with," the sergeant said.

"He's lying. He doesn't have the money."

"It appears that neither do you."

"$400,000 each," she offered.

The sergeant chuckled. "Our business is concluded."

He aimed his pistol and squeezed the trigger again. Another bullet rocketed across the living room and smacked into Skyler's chest. A geyser of blood erupted, and she fell to the tile. She gasped and gurgled for a moment, her body twitching before she finally went limp.

The sergeant looked at me. "For your sake, I hope you can do as you say."

50

"I'll need to make a phone call to transfer your funds," I said.

The sergeant thought about it for a moment, then nodded to one of his associates. An officer produced my phone, held it to my face, and the screen unlocked. I told him to contact Isabella.

He scrolled through my contact list and put the call on speakerphone.

Isabella's voice filtered through the living room. "I see you're in a bit of trouble."

The wireless security cameras that we had placed earlier were still in operation. Isabella had seen the whole thing and was monitoring the situation.

"Here's how this is going to work," she said. "I have the house under video surveillance. I can clearly see all of your faces, and my recognition software has identified you, Sergeant

Johnson, Officer Knowles, Officer Pinder, and Officer Williams."

Their eyes rounded, and they all exchanged worried glances.

"How does she know our names?" Pinder muttered to the sergeant.

"You're going to release Deputy Wild and the others. Then you and your friends are going to clean up the mess and walk out of the house. You'll forget this ever happened. If you don't do as I say, this footage will go public."

"You're bluffing," Sergeant Johnson said.

"Am I?"

That hung there for a moment.

Then all of their phones buzzed simultaneously with a text message. It contained a clip of the video feed from the camera we placed on the gate.

The faces of the cops went long when they watched it. There they were, doing bad things—all captured in 4K, ultra HD video. There was no mistaking Sergeant Johnson's murder of Skyler and Maverick.

"Smile for the camera, boys," Isabella said.

Sergeant Johnson grimaced.

"Now, you may think you have friends in high places, but I have friends in higher places. And if anything happens to my people in that house or anywhere else on that island, I will hunt each and every one of you down. Is that understood?"

There was a long moment of silence.

"How do we know you won't release the footage anyway?" Johnson asked.

"I'm a woman of my word."

"You expect me to trust you?"

"What choice do you have?"

"Maybe I kill them and hunt you down," he suggested.

Isabella laughed. "You're smarter than that, aren't you?"

He hesitated for a long moment.

Isabella proceeded to tell him his address, his wife's name, and how many kids he had. She went down the list, and it didn't take long for them to realize they were dealing with someone they didn't want to cross.

"Alright," Johnson said. He nodded to one of his associates.

Officer Pinder removed his weapon from Denise's head, and I breathed a sigh of relief.

Another goon uncuffed me, then Denise.

"I knew you'd make the right decision," Isabella said.

I took my phone from the goon.

"Don't forget to tidy up," Isabella warned.

The dirty cops exchanged a look.

The neighbors had undoubtedly heard gunshots and seen the patrol cars. There would be questions.

"Go!" the sergeant said to me.

I figured they'd stage the scene and make up some kind of story. I had no doubt there was jewelry, cash, and other valuables they could pocket for their troubles.

We gathered our belongings, and I fumbled through Maverick's pocket for his car keys before we hustled out of the house.

JD startled us as we exited. He had a pistol aimed at the doorway and quickly lowered it when we stepped out.

My face wrinkled with confusion. "How did you get out?"

"I was about to ask you the same thing." He grinned. "You're never going to believe this."

"Tell me on the way to the airport before they change their minds."

"I don't think I'm traveling with you guys anymore," Denise said as we hustled toward the red Mustang.

I chuckled.

We tossed our baggage in the trunk, and I climbed behind the wheel. JD hopped in the back, and Denise took the front seat.

I cranked up the engine, and we rolled out of the circular driveway past the fountain. I pulled onto the road and put the top down. A few curious neighbors still stood outside gossiping. One of them happened to be Veronica.

"Stop here," JD said.

He dropped the magazine from the pistol and ejected the round in the chamber. He handed the weapon back to Veronica.

Denise and I looked on with shock.

"Hi, Tyson," Veronica said with a cute smile and a wave like nothing had ever happened.

"Thanks," JD begrudgingly said.

"I'm really sorry about everything," Veronica said. "Sometimes I get a little carried away."

That was the understatement of the year.

"Are we cool now?" she asked.

"You're, uh... still wanted in the States," JD said. "But I'm not going to come after you."

She smiled. "It all worked out for the best. I met a great guy. We're going to get married." She muttered aside, "And he's loaded. I wish he was here now. You should meet him."

"Some other time," JD said. "Catch you later."

We drove away, and I waited for an explanation.

He shrugged. "She saw me in the back of the patrol car and let me out. Gave me a bobby pin to pick the cuffs and gave me the gun."

I laughed.

"How the hell did you two get out?" JD asked.

I told him the story.

The night air swirled, and I changed the radio station. Skyler and Maverick had horrible taste in music.

I called Isabella. "I guess I owe you one."

"I think we're even. I returned funds to everyone who had money invested on the exchange."

"You could have kept that money."

"You could have too," Isabella said. "Maybe there's hope for us yet."

I laughed and thanked her again for saving our lives. She told me a plane would be waiting at the FBO for us. We couldn't get back to Coconut Key fast enough.

I ended the call, leaned back in my seat, and let the wind blow through my hair. The stars flickered above, and the adrenaline began to dissipate. I wouldn't breathe easy until we were airborne.

The three of us celebrated our survival with a glass of whiskey on the flight back. Jack took the opportunity to regale Denise with the details of our adventure.

"I think that is the shortest vacation I've ever had. What am I going to tell the sheriff when I come back to work tomorrow?"

"Easy," JD said. "Just don't go to work for a few days. Lounge around. Pamper yourself. Go to the spa."

Denise rolled her eyes.

"I'll get you a cabana at the Seven Seas. You can unwind."

She lifted a curious eyebrow. "Good luck getting a room now. That place is booked solid." She paused. "I could just stay on the boat with you guys. You have guest staterooms. I could lounge around and do nothing all day. You could cook me breakfast. Pamper me. I'm traumatized. I need to be compensated."

I chuckled. "You were the one who wanted to tag along."

"Yeah, well. I didn't know it was going to be this bad."

"All's well that ends well," I said.

JD lifted his glass, and we toasted.

We touched down at the FBO in Coconut Key an hour later. Isabella had arranged a driver. He collected our baggage, and we piled into the limousine, sliding into the cushy leather seats.

I had to admit, having Denise around the *Avventura* for a few days wouldn't be a bad thing.

We returned to the marina and boarded the boat. It felt empty without Buddy and Fluffy. I had arranged for Teagan to look after them.

I showed Denise to her guest stateroom, and JD and I unpacked our things. We all had one more celebratory cocktail on the sky deck under the stars.

I got a text from Paris Delaney. *[I heard everyone that had funds on XTC got their money back. Did you have a hand in that?]*

[I can neither confirm nor deny.]

[Care to tell me the details of how something like that could have happened?]

[No.]

[You're no fun.]

[I think you know better.]

[I do.] She followed with a wink emoji.

I had an immense sense of gratitude. We'd cheated death once again. How many times can you tempt fate? I'm sure I was against my upper limit.

Daniels called the next morning. I grabbed the phone from the nightstand and swiped the screen. With a scratchy voice, I said, "What is it?"

"You two nitwits back in town?"

"Yeah."

"I figured. The return of those funds is all over the news."

"I'm not really sure how that happened," I said modestly.

"We got an anonymous tip. Lennox Bradley may be squatting on that abandoned cruise ship at Salt Point. Get over there and check it out. Take Erickson and Faulkner with you."

"How's Mendoza?"

"He had some internal hemorrhaging. They had to go back in. He's stable now. The sooner we can get Lennox Bradley behind bars, the better. I don't like people who shoot my deputies."

"I don't like them either."

"Speaking of Mendoza. The feds still haven't moved on the fraud case."

"Not surprising."

"Good news is that prepaid cellular found on Justin Smith at the time of his arrest was used to make several calls to another burner. I was able to get a warrant and track that second phone. Noah Benson screwed up. He turned the burner on while he was at home and it pinged the tower. That definitively connects him to Justin."

"That's great."

"It gets better. I guess a few days in lockup was enough to convince Justin to testify against Noah. He made a sworn affidavit implicating Noah in the conspiracy. Echols signed off on a warrant."

"Fantastic. When do we pick him up?"

"Well, it's not all sunshine and roses. Noah vanished. Hasn't shown up to the office. Looks like he left his place in a hurry. His personal and company funds have been moved to an offshore account. You're gonna have to track that son-of-a-bitch down. You're good at that type of thing."

"I'm on it."

I ended the call, climbed out of bed, and went through my morning routine. I banged on the hatch to JD's VIP stateroom and told him we had bad guys to catch.

Ready for more?

The adventure continues with Wild Massacre!

Join my newsletter and find out what happens next!

AUTHOR'S NOTE

Thanks for taking this incredible journey with me. I'm having such a blast writing about Tyson and JD, and I've got plenty more adventures to come. I hope you'll stick around for the wild ride.

Thanks for all the great reviews and kind words!

If you liked this book, let me know with a review on Amazon.

Thanks for reading!

—Tripp

TYSON WILD

Wild Ocean

Wild Justice

Wild Rivera

Wild Tide

Wild Rain

Wild Captive

Wild Killer

Wild Honor

Wild Gold

Wild Case

Wild Crown

Wild Break

Wild Fury

Wild Surge

Wild Impact

Wild L.A.

Wild High

Wild Abyss

Wild Life

Wild Spirit

Wild Thunder

Wild Season

Wild Rage

Wild Heart

Wild Spring

Wild Outlaw

Wild Revenge

Wild Secret

Wild Envy

Wild Surf

Wild Venom

Wild Island

Wild Demon

Wild Blue

Wild Lights

Wild Target

Wild Jewel

Wild Greed

Wild Sky

Wild Storm

Wild Bay

Wild Chaos

Wild Cruise

Wild Catch

Wild Encounter

Wild Blood

Wild Vice

Wild Winter

Wild Malice

Wild Fire

Wild Deceit

Wild Massacre

Wild...

CONNECT WITH ME

I'm just a geek who loves to write. Follow me on Facebook.

www.trippellis.com